"I'M SORRY, MRS. DAWSON," I SAID, "BUT I AM NOT GOING TO THE CIRCUS. I CHOOSE TO STAY IN SCHOOL."

"I'm not going either," David said.

Other voices joined in.

"I don't like this circus."

"I'd rather stay here than support people who are mean to animals."

"My dad said I don't have to go."

"If you did not plan to go," Mrs. Dawson said, "why did you turn in your signed permission slips?"

"Because you said you would lower my grade by a full point if I didn't turn in the slip," David said.

At that, Dr. Martinez made a choking sound. He said, "Anyone who wishes to skip the circus and remain in school may do so."

Mrs. Dawson looked as if she were about to cry. She turned to me and said, "Our happy day is spoiled. You let your personal feelings ruin the reward that the whole class earned."

She turned and marched out of the classroom. Mrs. Gummer and Flora followed her.

The last one in line, Pinkie, hesitated at the door and then returned to his seat.

"I never thought I would stay in school if I didn't have to," Pinkie said, "but you are right about this, and Mrs. Dawson is wrong."

When Pinkie plopped down at his desk, I felt like cheering.

Books by Peg Kehret

Cages
Danger at the Fair
Deadly Stranger
Horror at the Haunted House
Night of Fear
Nightmare Mountain
Sisters, Long Ago
The Richest Kids in Town
Terror at the Zoo
FRIGHTMARES™: Cat Burglar on the Prowl
FRIGHTMARES™: Bone Breath and the Vandals
FRIGHTMARES™: Don't Go Near Mrs. Tallie
FRIGHTMARES™: Desert Danger
FRIGHTMARES™: The Ghost Followed Us Home
FRIGHTMARES™: Race to Disaster
FRIGHTMARES™: Screaming Eagles
FRIGHTMARES™: Backstage Fright
The Blizzard Disaster
The Flood Disaster
The Volcano Disaster
The Secret Journey
My Brother Made Me Do It
The Hideout
Saving Lilly

Published by Simon & Schuster

Saving Lilly

Peg Kehret

Aladdin Paperbacks
New York London Toronto Sydney Singapore

First Aladdin Paperbacks edition November 2002

ALADDIN PAPERBACKS
An imprint of Simon & Schuster
Children's Publishing Division
1230 Avenue of the Americas
New York, NY 10020

Also available in a Minstrel Books hardcover edition.

Printed in the United States of America
10 9 8 7 6 5 4 3 2

Library of Congress Control Number 2001098470
ISBN 0-671-03423-5 (Aladdin pbk.)

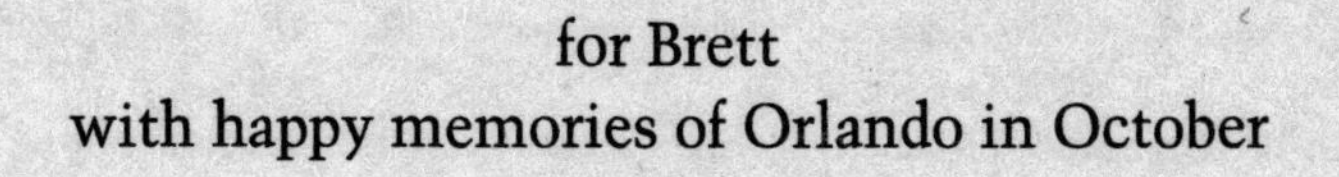

for Brett
with happy memories of Orlando in October

Contents

1

The Three Hundred Books Challenge

Not many sixth graders get an opportunity to save an elephant. I had that chance, and it turned out to be the biggest challenge of my life.

The first time I saw Lilly, chains circled her ankles. She moved—slowly, as if it hurt her to walk—down the ramp of the small circus trailer that had brought her to town.

By then I was already in big trouble with my teacher. Some troubles are easily solved and quickly forgotten, but this one wasn't. The trouble I had with Mrs. Dawson led me to Lilly, and changed me forever.

It all began one drowsy Monday in late April. The sun streamed through the school's windows, making it impossible to think of anything except baseball, swimming, and summer vacation. I wanted to stretch out in a sunny spot the way my cat, Beanie, does and snooze.

I was amusing myself by writing my name, Erin Wrenn, in the middle of a piece of paper and then drawing flowers around it, when Mrs. Dawson rapped a ruler against the edge of her desk.

"I have a challenge for you," she announced.

Surprised, I quit drawing daisies and looked at my teacher. The rest of the class paid attention, too. We were not used to surprises. I liked Mrs. Dawson, but most of the time her class was boring. She spent twenty years teaching kindergarten, then switched to sixth grade this year. She probably should have stayed with kindergarten.

"I challenge you," Mrs. Dawson said, "to read three hundred books before May tenth."

Pinkie Ensburg, who sits behind me and is not exactly the world's greatest scholar, gave a little yelp, as if someone had stepped on his toes. "No way," Pinkie said. "I probably won't read three hundred books in my entire life."

"Not three hundred books each," Mrs. Dawson said. "Three hundred total. There are twenty-eight students in this class; if you each read eleven books, you'll be over the goal."

Flora Gummer said, "I will be glad to read eleven books before May tenth, Mrs. Dawson."

Behind me, Pinkie pretended to gag.

"If you do it," Mrs. Dawson told the class, "the prize will be a special field trip."

David Showers, who lives next door to me and is

my best friend, leaned across the aisle and whispered, "Our TAG project will take a lot of time this week. Do you think we can do that and read extra books, too?"

David and I attend TAG class two mornings a week. TAG stands for Talented and Gifted, although privately we say it means Time Away from Gummer. Flora drives us crazy with her goody-goody comments. Except for recess, TAG is my favorite part of school.

Our TAG assignment was to write a report on animals in circuses. We were supposed to tell how they are cared for, their training, what laws are meant to protect them, and how those laws are enforced.

David and I didn't choose the subject; Mrs. Mapes, our TAG teacher, assigned it. She said she knew we liked animals and, since a circus would be coming to Harborview soon, the topic was timely.

I whispered back, "The reading we do for TAG can count for the class challenge, too."

We had known about the TAG project for nearly a month but, as usual, we had waited until the last week to begin. David says he does his best work under pressure; I procrastinate because I'd rather read or play with Beanie than start a big research project.

"Are there any questions about my challenge?" Mrs. Dawson said.

"Do the books have to be a minimum length?" Pinkie asked.

I wouldn't put it past Pinkie to try to get credit for reading *Goodnight, Moon* or *Pat the Bunny.*

"There are no rules about length or type of book," Mrs. Dawson replied, "but I trust you will not read any picture books meant for preschoolers and try to have them count toward the total."

"If someone reads more than eleven, can I read fewer?" Pinkie asked. "Or do we each have to read the same number?"

Mrs. Dawson sighed. "The total is what counts," she said. "However, I hope that each of you will want to contribute your fair share."

Pinkie poked me in the back to get my attention, then leaned forward and whispered, "You're a good reader, Erin. You can read twenty books and I'll read two."

"Thanks a lot, Pinkie," I said.

I was surprised he offered to read any at all. If Pinkie would spend as much time doing his schoolwork as he spends thinking of ways to avoid doing any schoolwork, he wouldn't be on the verge of being held back in sixth grade.

"All those in favor of accepting my challenge, raise your hand," Mrs. Dawson said.

David and I raised our hands. So did the rest of the students. Even Pinkie voted yes, although I knew he had no intention of reading eleven books before May tenth or any other time.

"When you finish a book," Mrs. Dawson said,

"write the title and author on a piece of paper and give it to me. I made a chart to keep track of the total books read."

She taped a large graph to the bulletin board next to her desk. Across the top it said THE 300 BOOKS CHALLENGE. Below that, from left to right, were the numbers 0 to 300. Dates, starting with the next day's date at the bottom, went up the left side, ending with May tenth at the top.

"Where will we go on the field trip?" David asked.

"That's a secret," Mrs. Dawson said. "First you have to read the three hundred books; then I'll tell you our destination."

"Stay tuned to learn how a sixth-grade class earned a personal tour of the sewage treatment plant," David said.

Jason snickered. Randy and Scooter groaned. Andrea said, "Yuck." Mrs. Dawson ignored the remark.

I laughed. David plans to be a TV news broadcaster and he often creates "teasers" that are supposed to make people watch the news.

"I'm sure whatever Mrs. Dawson chooses will be educational and wonderful," said Flora.

"I don't care if we go to the dump," Pinkie said, "as long as it gets me out of school for a few hours."

"I guarantee it will be someplace fun and exciting," Mrs. Dawson said. Then she used her fake voice that always sounds as if she's talking to a group of six-year-olds. "Reading three hundred books will be fun and exciting, too," she chirped.

"Not for me," muttered Pinkie.

The challenge *would* be fun for me—I love to read—but I didn't say so. Other kids sometimes resent it when the schoolwork that they are struggling with is easy for me, so I try hard to blend in and be like everyone else.

Mrs. Dawson told us we could all go to the school library to select books to read, and there was a general stampede toward the door.

I checked out five books—three mysteries, which I love, and two books about circuses. That night Mom drove David and me to the public library to get more material about circus animals.

For the rest of that week, all I did outside of school was work on the TAG project. Well, almost all. I went to my final softball game (I got a single and struck out twice), and I played mouse-on-a-string with Beanie every night.

Mouse-on-a-string is his favorite game. I had tied a long piece of string around a catnip mouse. When I pull the string to make the mouse move, Beanie chases and attacks the mouse. He gets so excited that he always makes me laugh. It doesn't take much to make a cat happy.

Every night after dinner, David came over to work with me. After a few hours of research we began to wish we had been assigned a different subject.

My feelings for animals run deep, and what we

learned made me sick to my stomach. I could hardly believe how badly animals are sometimes treated just so their owners can make a bigger profit.

David likes animals, too; he has a dog, Snoopy, and two gerbils, Lucy and Linus. When we read how rope is tied around the tigers' necks and the animals are choked to make them obey, David got so angry that he kicked the desk. I felt a horrified sadness, as if I personally knew each of the creatures who were mistreated.

We soon had a pile of printouts from web sites such as the Fund for Animals and the American Society for the Prevention of Cruelty to Animals. We had pamphlets and fact sheets about individual circuses and several quotations from the books we had read.

With so much material, writing our report was a cinch. We wrote twelve pages about the miserable lives of circus animals—two more pages than required.

Because Mrs. Mapes always likes posters or charts, we decided to make a poster of a tiger jumping through a hoop of fire. Across the top we wrote ALL ANIMALS NATURALLY FEAR FIRE and across the bottom we wrote THIS TIGER FEARS PUNISHMENT FROM HIS TRAINER EVEN MORE.

Beanie jumped in my lap as I used a bright red marker to highlight the flames. I rubbed behind Beanie's ears the way he likes. As he purred and pushed his head under my chin, my heart ached for all the unfortunate animals who are forced to leave their natural habitats and made to perform for humans.

It isn't right, I thought, but what could a twelve-year-old do about it?

At nine o'clock Thursday night, David and I finished our TAG project. We celebrated with bowls of strawberry ice cream.

"My family went to a fair once," David said as we ate, "and we saw a dancing bear. At the time I thought it was wonderful. Now I wonder how that bear was trained to dance. Did he get beaten if he didn't put his front legs in the air and keep them there?"

"Probably," I said. "Bears in the wild don't dance around on their hind legs."

"That bear should have been walking on all four feet, in the forest where he belongs. But we didn't think about that, so we paid money to see him dance, which is exactly what the bear's trainer wanted."

David looked so sad and guilty that I said, "You didn't know. You'll never go to anything like that again, now that you know how the animals are trained."

"That's for sure," David said.

"I will never attend a fair or circus or any other event that's mean to animals," I vowed.

"Neither will I," David said.

He stuck out his hand and I shook it solemnly, as if we were making a legal pact.

I stirred my ice cream into strawberry soup.

"I've always wanted to be a veterinarian," I said, "so I could help animals. Now I wonder if I could help them more if I became a lawyer and worked for new laws to protect animals."

David announced, "We interrupt this program with breaking news: the Supreme Court ruled today that all animals have legal rights. After talented young attorney Erin Wrenn electrified the courtroom with her eloquent closing statements, the Court's decision was unanimous."

"Details in ten years," I said, wishing I were already grown up and could help the animals now.

"The Chief Justice praised Ms. Wrenn for her passion, insight, and dedication," David continued. "Ms. Wrenn responded that she owes her fondness for animals to her childhood friend, Beanie, who licked the ice cream when she wasn't watching."

When I realized what David had said, I plucked Beanie from the table, where he had his head in my dish, and plopped him on the floor.

2

A Terrible Surprise

Did you like your topic?" Mrs. Mapes asked, when David and I turned in our report.

"No," I said. "I felt sick when I learned how the animals are mistreated."

"Good," she said. "That means it made you think."

"It made me think," I said, "that there are some mean people in the world and I'd like to lock them all in jail."

"We need tougher laws to protect the animals," David said.

"If you want to change how animals are treated," Mrs. Mapes said, "you must educate people."

"How?" David asked. "I can't go up to people on the street and say, 'Excuse me, did you know that circus bears sometimes have their paws burned to force them to stand on their hind legs?'"

"No, you can't," Mrs. Mapes agreed. "But once you have knowledge yourself, you'll find opportunities to share it."

Since it was Friday, Mrs. Dawson let us have free reading time most of the afternoon. Before we went home, we gave her the titles of the books we had finished.

We watched as she extended the red line on the chart, stopping at forty-one.

"You'll need to be over one hundred by Monday morning," she said, "or you'll never make your goal."

I read five books that weekend. Mom took me to the public library on Saturday because I could tell I was going to finish everything I had checked out from school.

My total might have been six except my sister, Kathleen, came into the den on Sunday afternoon when I was curled up in Dad's big chair with Beanie on my lap and my nose in another mystery.

Kathleen carried a notebook and pencil. "What would you do if you were president of the United States?" she asked.

"What contest are you entering this time?" I asked.

Kathleen, who is in tenth grade, is always making up jingles or slogans for contests, in hopes of winning a fantastic prize. She's been entering contests for two years. So far she's won an electric toothbrush and a year's supply of jelly beans—not from the same contest.

"Free jelly beans!" Kathleen had yelled, when she opened the letter about her prize. "I've won a year's supply of free jelly beans!"

I have to admit the jelly beans were a great prize, especially since Mom and Dad made her share them, but they really weren't free. Kathleen spends hours working on each contest entry, plus it costs postage to mail all of them.

Most of the time she doesn't win anything. If she had spent the same amount of time baby-sitting that she spent entering contests last year, she could have purchased the toothbrush and the jelly beans and had plenty of money left over.

"I'm writing fifty words about What I Would Do if I Were President of the United States," Kathleen said. "I thought you might have a good idea."

"I'd lower the voting age to twelve," I suggested.

"Be serious."

"Make stronger penalties for people who mistreat animals."

"Good." Kathleen wrote that down. "What else?"

"Get rid of circuses that have wild animal acts such as tigers and elephants, and make it illegal to import those animals."

"I only have fifty words," Kathleen said, "and I want to include other stuff besides animals. What about nuclear weapons? What about foreign policy?"

"You asked what I would do if I were president," I said. "I care more about animals than I care about foreign policy."

"You can have ten of the fifty words," Kathleen said. "Figure out what you want to say about animals, and I'll make that part of my entry."

"What's the prize this time?" I asked.

"Money," Kathleen said. "Lots of money."

I was unimpressed. Money had been the prize in the toothbrush contest, too, but only one person got the ten-thousand-dollar first-prize jackpot. The other winners, like Kathleen, got an electric toothbrush.

On the other hand, there was always the slim chance that Kathleen would actually win. "If you win do I get twenty percent?" I asked.

"Why would I give you twenty percent of my prize?"

"Because ten words is twenty percent of your entry."

Kathleen thought for a moment. "It's a deal," she said.

It took me most of the afternoon to write my ten words. It's harder to write a good short sentence than a good long one. I finally decided on *Ban exotic animal acts. Make harsher penalties for animal abusers.* I gave Kathleen my final effort and she agreed to use it in her entry.

* * *

First thing Monday morning Mrs. Dawson collected our lists of the books we had read. When she added my five books to the total, Pinkie poked me and whispered, "Way to go, Erin. If you keep that up I won't have to read any books."

Lots of other kids had done extra reading that weekend, too. David had three books on his list.

The longest list of all was from Flora Gummer, who had read eight books. Personally, I think she cheated and put down books she had already read before Mrs. Dawson announced the challenge. Either that or she didn't sleep for two days.

When Mrs. Dawson added up all the titles, our class had read ninety-two books over the weekend, for a total of one hundred and thirty-three books. She drew a big red line on the chart from forty-one on Friday to one hundred thirty-three that morning.

Everyone clapped, then Mrs. Dawson let us go to the library again to return the books we had read and to check out others. Even Pinkie checked out a book that time. It's a wonder the librarian didn't faint.

By the next Friday I had finished two more books, and our class total was up to one hundred seventy-five.

At recess, we guessed possible destinations for the mystery field trip.

"I think it will be a picnic at Harborview Park," said David.

"Maybe Mrs. Dawson will take us to Disney World," said Flora.

"Disney World is too far away," I said, "and too expensive." For someone who could read eight books in one weekend, Flora didn't have much sense.

"If I thought the prize was Disney World," said Pinkie, "I would read some books."

"I'm going to read all weekend," I told David as we walked home together on Friday.

"I have a game tomorrow," he said, "but I'll read as much as I can." David plays softball on a parks department team. I played on a team, too, but my season was over.

As soon as I got home, I cleaned up my room so Mom wouldn't nag me about it. I played mouse-on-a-string with Beanie, unloaded the dishwasher (my job after school every day) and settled into Dad's big chair with my stack of books.

When Kathleen came in to ask if I would help her think of sixteen ways to use Soapy Suds detergent, I shook my head.

I was determined not to be distracted from my goal, which was to finish six more books before Monday morning.

I had to skip all of my favorite weekend TV shows and I turned down a chance to go to a movie with Aunt Lorna, but I read all six books. That brought my personal total to thirteen books, which

I figured was eleven for my share and two for Pinkie.

The room buzzed with anticipation on Monday morning as we all told one another how many books we had read. I tried to add the total in my head, but I kept getting interrupted.

As soon as the Pledge of Allegiance was over, Mrs. Dawson said, "Did you read over the weekend?"

"Yes! Yes!" Everyone waved slips of paper in the air, eager to know the total.

Mrs. Dawson collected the lists and read each one out loud as she wrote down the numbers.

"David Showers—four books."

"Flora Gummer—five books."

"Erin Wrenn—six books."

"Pinkie Ensburg—two books."

Mrs. Dawson got all excited when she said Pinkie's name. I don't think he had ever read anything on his own before.

I turned and gave Pinkie a double high-five, and his face glowed like a neon sign. I realized it had probably been harder for him to read two books than it had been for me to read six.

"What's the total?" David asked.

Mrs. Dawson's fingers tapped her calculator. "Three hundred fourteen!"

"We did it!" Andrea said.

Pinkie pounded on his desk; everyone else cheered and stomped the floor.

"A group of students astonished their teacher by reading three hundred books," David said. "Find out how they did it, on the noon news today."

We didn't quiet down until Mrs. Dawson said, "Your surprise field trip will be next Thursday."

We quit congratulating each other and listened.

"Our entire class," Mrs. Dawson said, "is going to the circus!"

Most of the kids said, "Cool!" or "All right!"

David and I looked at each other. I knew that the concern I saw on his face was a reflection of my own worried expression.

I put my hand in the air.

"Yes, Erin?" Mrs. Dawson said.

"Which circus is it?"

"It's called the Glitter Tent Circus. This is the first time it has come to Harborview."

I remembered reading about the Glitter Tent Circus when we did our research, but I couldn't recall what I had read. Maybe it was one of the circuses that used only human performers.

"Their ads look wonderful," Mrs. Dawson added. "There are trapeze artists and dancing bears and jugglers and an elephant that does tricks and clowns and even a tiger who jumps through a hoop of fire!"

I looked at David again. He shook his head sadly. I felt a nervous knot in my stomach. I am not used to telling a teacher that I don't want to do what she expects me to do.

"I can't go to the circus," I said.

The whole class looked at me.

"Can't go?" Mrs. Dawson said. "Why not? If you have a dentist appointment that day, I'm sure it could be changed."

I have braces on my teeth, and occasionally I get excused from school to go to the orthodontist.

Before I could say that I did not have a dental appointment, David said, "I can't go, either."

Mrs. Dawson's eyes narrowed, as if she suspected we were playing a practical joke on her.

"David and I studied about circus animals for a TAG project," I explained, "and we object to the way the animals are treated."

"You don't know anything about this circus," Mrs. Dawson said. "What makes you assume the animals are mistreated?"

"If the circus has bears, an elephant, and a tiger doing tricks, we know all we need to know," David said.

"Animals don't do such unnatural things," I explained, "unless they are forced to do them. Trainers beat the animals or use painful tools to make them perform."

My voice trembled and the other kids stared at me as if I were a freak.

"Gross," said Andrea.

"The circus is fine family entertainment," Mrs. Dawson said, "and you should be thrilled at this chance to attend it for free. The only reason we can do this is that my nephew is president of the Harborview County Fair Board and the circus will be held at the fairgrounds. He was given a block of tickets, which he kindly passed along to me."

"Could you ask your nephew to investigate this circus?" I asked. "He could easily find out whether they violate the animal welfare laws."

Mrs. Dawson was not listening. "When I was a girl," she said softly, "the circus came to town once a year, and my grandpa always took me." She smiled over our heads, as if she were seeing herself as a child. "I looked forward to it for months and I was never disappointed. It was the best day of the entire summer."

I looked down at my desk. Don't make waves, I told myself. Why get in trouble with my teacher when there's nothing I can do about the plight of the animals, anyway?

"The circus sounds wonderful, Mrs. Dawson," Flora said.

No, it doesn't, I thought. *It sounds horrible.*

3

Circus Facts

During lunch hour David and I logged on to the Internet. We looked at a web site that lists circuses and tells whether they've ever been cited for mistreating animals. If they have, it tells when and what happened.

When we clicked on the Glitter Tent Circus, a long list of violations of the animal welfare law appeared on the monitor.

"Oh, no," I said.

"They're one of the worst circuses," David said.

We printed out the list.

Facts About the Glitter Tent Circus

The Glitter Tent Circus has been cited by the U.S. Department of Agriculture as follows:

1. When a lion broke her leg, the trainer did not have a veterinarian check her.

2. Glitter Tent Circus employees failed to provide nutritious food to the point where some animals suffered from malnutrition. They gave the animals dirty water to drink.

3. The trainers confined lions and tigers in their small travel cages for nine straight days without letting them out to exercise. The cages were filthy.

4. Painful bullhooks are used to control the elephant.

5. A pony was being ridden even though he had open saddle sores. The sores were not being treated.

6. Trainers did not hose down the sea lions to keep them wet during travel. Four sea lions died.

7. Animals were kept in full sun during 95-degree weather, without access to shade or water.

8. Witnesses saw a trainer beating a tiger with a heavy rod. Later the tiger appeared unable to properly focus his eyes, and missed the pedestal he was supposed to jump on.

Conclusion:

Glitter Tent Circus does not meet even the minimum standards of animal care.

"Now what are we going to do?" David asked.

"We'll show this list to Mrs. Dawson. When she sees how often the Glitter Tent Circus has been in trouble for not taking care of their animals, she'll change her mind and choose a different field trip."

We went back to class early hoping to talk to Mrs. Dawson alone.

No such luck. Flora Gummer was already there.

"Do you really object to the circus," Flora asked, "because animals do tricks?"

"Yes," I said.

"That is the dumbest thing I ever heard of," Flora said. "What's wrong with teaching animals to do tricks? I taught my dog to shake hands and roll over and he really likes to do it. Maybe the circus animals like to do tricks, too."

"How did you teach him to shake hands and roll over?" I asked.

"Every time he does it right, I give him a treat and tell him he's a good dog."

"Your dog does the tricks," I said, "because he likes the treats and the praise you give him."

"So what's bad about that?" Flora said.

"Nothing," David said. "The tricks you taught your dog don't hurt him and you don't make him do anything he's afraid to do. In between tricks he isn't locked in a cage. There's a big difference between that and what happens in the circus."

"Instead of treats and praise," I said, "circus trainers use electric prods and whips and long poles with sharp hooks on the ends. Sometimes the animals' teeth are removed."

"You know what your problem is?" Flora asked.

"What?" I said.

"You know too much."

Mrs. Dawson arrived then. I hoped Flora would leave, but of course she hung around and listened.

I handed Mrs. Dawson the list that we had printed out. "Here is a list of the citations that the Glitter Tent Circus has received," I said.

"Where did you get this?"

"There's a web site that tells about circuses."

Mrs. Dawson laid the page on her desk without reading it.

"I saw my nephew last night," she said. "He showed me a publicity release from the circus manager. It says that the purpose of the Glitter Tent Circus is to educate the public about exotic animals such as tigers and elephants which are not native to this area."

"Educate the public?" I said. "By beating the animals and not feeding them properly?"

"I think you've been taken in by some misguided animal rights activists," Mrs. Dawson said, "and I don't want to hear any more about it." She turned away from us and began straightening some papers on her desk.

Flora smirked.

I didn't know what to do next. Mrs. Dawson had not even read the list of violations that the Glitter Tent Circus was guilty of. How could we change her mind if she didn't want to know the facts?

The rest of the students began arriving.

David got some pushpins and put our facts about the Glitter Tent Circus on the bulletin board where student work is displayed.

"If that is your TAG project," Mrs. Dawson said, "you may turn it in to your TAG teacher."

"We've already turned in our TAG project," I said. "This is information for the class."

Mrs. Dawson took down the list. "I'll keep this for you until school is out today," she said. "Then you may take it home."

"You aren't going to let us share what we've learned?" David said.

"I am not going to let you spoil a wonderful field trip for our class. You have no proof that the Glitter Tent Circus mistreats its animals. Just because something appears on the Internet doesn't make it true."

I had never argued with a teacher before but I was so upset, I blurted: "Every one of those citations is documented by the U.S. Department of Agriculture. No one would dare to make such accusations without proof; the circus would sue them if these things weren't true."

The bell rang.

"Take your seats, please," Mrs. Dawson said.

I sat down. So did the rest of the class.

I clenched my teeth angrily. How could Mrs. Dawson say we had no proof when the proof was right there in front of her?

Pinkie whispered in my ear, "Whooee! I never thought I'd hear the smartest girl in school talk back to a teacher."

I ignored him. Being smart is good for tests and grades but it isn't always good for fitting in. I often feel different from other kids because I can figure things out more quickly than they can and I'm bored by the TV shows that most of them watch, but I always keep my mouth shut and try to seem like everyone else.

The rest of the morning I debated what to do. I could say nothing more about the circus, then pretend to be sick on the day of the field trip. Mom would let me stay home. That would avoid another clash with Mrs. Dawson, my classmates would think I was normal, and I would not have to watch the circus animals perform.

If I pretend to be sick, I thought, it will seem as if I approve of the circus, and I can't do that.

Once when Beanie was still a kitten, my little cousin, Misty, picked him up by his tail. "Put him down!" I demanded. Instead she began swinging him around, so I ran to her and made her release him.

Misty went crying to Aunt Lorna and I expected

Aunt Lorna to scold me, but she didn't. She said, "Good for you, Erin. Beanie can't speak for himself, so it's up to you to defend him."

The circus animals can't speak for themselves, either, I thought. I have to do what I believe is right.

Some of the kids might think I was weird for taking a stand, and Mrs. Dawson would be unhappy, but somehow I had to keep my class from attending the circus.

I didn't get a chance to talk to David until after school.

"Can you believe her?" he sputtered. "She isn't even going to ask her nephew about that list of violations. Her mind is made up about the circus and she's determined not to let the truth change her opinion."

"She doesn't have to change her opinion," I said. "We can't educate Mrs. Dawson if she doesn't want to learn, but we can tell the other kids what we know."

David waited for me to continue.

"We're going to circulate a petition," I said. "We'll tell our classmates how the circus animals are treated and ask them to sign a request that we go somewhere else for our field trip."

"If enough kids sign," David said, "Mrs. Dawson will have to change her plans."

"Exactly."

"A local girl was declared a genius today," David said, "after concocting a brilliant strategy to avoid the circus. Meet this talented young woman and hear her plan at eleven tonight."

I didn't feel like a genius; I felt nervous, as if I were plunging down a one-way path without knowing where it led.

"Let's write the petition now," I said. "We can collect signatures tomorrow."

It was harder to write the petition than we had thought it would be. Like Kathleen's contest entries, we had to give a lot of information in as few words as possible.

After three hours and two bowls of Rocky Road ice cream each, we finally finished.

> We the undersigned object to the Glitter Tent Circus because this circus does not meet minimal federal standards for animal care. This circus has been cited many times by the United States Department of Agriculture for failing to provide proper veterinary care, nutritious food, clean water, and adequate exercise for its animals. Cruelty charges have been filed against their animal trainers. Therefore we request that our sixth grade class not attend the circus but have a different field trip instead.

We had twenty-eight lines where people could sign their names. I wrote my name on the first line and David wrote his on the second line.

"How many kids do you think will sign?" David asked.

"I'm betting most of them will after we show them the information we have."

"Let's make copies of the fact sheet," David suggested. "We can give those out when we pass around the petition."

We rode our bikes to the office supply store and made thirty copies of the fact sheet.

As soon as we began handing out fact sheets at recess the next day, we were surrounded by curious students who wanted to know where we had gotten the information and what we planned to do next.

I showed them the petition. "We're going to ask Mrs. Dawson to select a different field trip," I said. "If enough kids sign this petition, she'll have to change her mind."

Soon the whole playground was buzzing with talk of how the Glitter Tent Circus people were mean to their animals.

The playground supervisor, Mrs. Lorel, came over to see what all the commotion was about. I told her about the field trip that Mrs. Dawson had planned. Then I showed her the fact sheet about the Glitter Tent Circus. She read it.

"Did Mrs. Dawson say you can distribute this?" she asked.

"No," I said, "but she didn't say we can't, either."

"In other words, she doesn't know you're doing this. Is that right?"

I nodded. "We gave her this list yesterday but she wouldn't read it," I said, "and when we put it on the student bulletin board she took it down."

"So it's safe to assume she would not approve of your handing out copies during recess."

"How else are people going to learn the truth?" I asked.

"If these are true facts," Mrs. Lorel said, "then I don't want to attend that circus and I don't think your class should go, either. But you should not be doing this without your teacher's permission. I have no choice but to take this paper to her and tell her what you're doing."

4

Trouble with Mrs. Dawson

When recess ended David and I hung back, reluctant to face Mrs. Dawson.

We were the last two students to go inside. Mrs. Dawson was waiting for us with the fact sheet in her hand.

"I told you yesterday that you were to take this propaganda home," she said.

I didn't answer.

"Why didn't you tell me that you were going to give out copies of this?" she asked.

I looked at David.

"Erin, I am asking *you,*" Mrs. Dawson said. "Why didn't you tell me what you were going to do?"

"I knew you would tell us not to," I said.

"In other words, you deliberately hid what you were doing because you knew you were not supposed to do it."

I could feel twenty-six pairs of eyes boring into me, as the other kids hung on every word. My face felt hot, and I knew it was turning red, the way it always does when I get angry or embarrassed.

"We didn't hide what we were doing," I said. "We were standing right there on the playground."

"We have a right to free speech," David said.

"When you are at school," Mrs. Dawson said, "you are expected to obey the teachers. As long as you are in my class, I am in charge and you are to follow my rules."

"All we're asking is that the other kids be allowed to know the truth about the Glitter Tent Circus and then make up their own minds whether or not they want to go," I said.

"You are trying to brainwash your classmates. The truth is that the circus is exciting, fun entertainment."

"Not for the animals," I said.

You could have heard a mouse tiptoe across that classroom floor as everyone waited to hear Mrs. Dawson's reaction.

"Go to the principal's office," Mrs. Dawson said. "Both of you."

"Won't you at least read our list and our petition first?" I asked. "The circus might be different now than it was when you were a little girl."

It was the wrong thing to say. Mrs. Dawson's eyes flashed angrily. She pointed to the door. "I'll let Dr. Martinez know that you are coming," she said.

David and I left, walking silently toward the office.

The school secretary looked up when we entered. "Dr. Martinez wants you to wait here. He'll be with you in a few minutes."

We sat down.

"I've never been sent to the principal," David said. "Have you?"

"No," I said, "but I came close once. When I was in first grade, there was a stray dog on the playground one day. The janitor tied it up and called animal control. I heard him tell someone that the dog would be picked up and taken to the pound, so I sneaked out of class, went outside, and untied the dog. Then I hid in the girls' bathroom until lunchtime. I never got caught, but for the next month I was scared that I would be sent to the principal, kicked out of school, and disowned by my parents."

Those old nervous feelings returned as I sat beside David. I could imagine Mom's reaction if the principal called to tell her I had disobeyed my teacher.

The door to the principal's office opened and Dr. Martinez motioned us inside. He closed the door behind us and told us to sit in the two chairs that faced his desk.

"Now then, Erin and David," he said. "What's this all about? Mrs. Dawson tells me you are disrupting the class and refusing to go on a special field trip."

The words tumbled out. "David and I love animals," I said, "and when we did a TAG project about how cruelly some circus animals are treated, it made us furious. We promised each other we would never attend any event where exotic animals are forced to perform. Now Mrs. Dawson says we have to go to the circus."

"This circus has been cited many times for animal cruelty," David said. He handed Dr. Martinez our list of the circus's violations, and the petition, which now had six signatures besides our own.

Dr. Martinez listened carefully. He read the entire fact sheet and asked where we had gotten it. He read the petition.

"I am proud of you both for taking a stand for something you believe in," he said. "However, I can't let you distribute this information and circulate your petition on school property after your teacher has specifically asked you not to."

I glanced at David. He was staring at his shoes.

Dr. Martinez continued. "I will speak to Mrs. Dawson about the possibility of offering an alternative field trip for those who do not want to attend the circus. If she agrees to do that, and if there are some parent volunteers who will chaperon the second trip, then perhaps we can settle this matter to everyone's satisfaction."

"What if she won't offer a second field trip?" I asked.

Dr. Martinez thought for a moment. "I can't force her to plan a second trip if she does not want to do so," he said. "Mrs. Dawson has taught here for a long time. She's a dedicated, sincere woman and I will back up whatever decision she makes."

"Even if she's wrong?" I said.

"She believes she is right."

I didn't know what else to say. All we could do was hope that when Dr. Martinez asked Mrs. Dawson to offer a choice of field trips, she would agree to do it.

"When will you talk to her?" David asked.

Dr. Martinez said, "Today. You are excused to go back to class."

Instead of going back to our class, David and I went to the cafeteria and sat on the stage, behind the curtain. Neither of us could stand to face Mrs. Dawson quite yet.

"I think Dr. Martinez agrees with us about the circus," I said, "but he doesn't want to overrule Mrs. Dawson."

"I hope he can convince her," David said. "She'll probably say there isn't enough time to plan a second trip."

"Why don't we offer to plan the other field trip?" I

said. "If Mrs. Dawson didn't have to do any work, she'd have no reason to refuse."

"Let's do it," David said. "Where shall we go?"

"Someplace that doesn't cost anything."

"How about a picnic at Harborview Park? We can watch the boats and play ball."

"Perfect." I stood up and headed back to class. Now that we had a workable plan, I was ready to see Mrs. Dawson again.

We got to our classroom just as Mrs. Dawson was starting a spelling test. We slipped into our seats.

Pinkie poked me in the back. "What happened?" he whispered. "Did Dr. Martinez yell at you? Did you get detention?"

I shook my head and didn't answer. I wasn't going to get in trouble for talking during a spelling test. I had enough trouble with Mrs. Dawson already.

Shortly before the bell rang for lunch, Dr. Martinez came into our classroom. David and I did not leave with the rest of the kids.

I said, "We'd like to be in charge of a different field trip for any kids who don't want to go to the circus."

Mrs. Dawson glared at me.

"We could take sack lunches to Harborview Park," I said. "My mom doesn't work that day and I'm sure she would drive."

"If there are too many kids for one car," David said, "I'll see if my dad would go. He has a flexible schedule and maybe he could go to work early that day."

"We'll consider your offer," Dr. Martinez said. "Now I need to speak with Mrs. Dawson alone."

David and I walked into the hall. I wanted to stand outside the room and try to hear what was said but David tugged at my sleeve and motioned for me to move along.

When we reached the cafeteria, several kids came to our table to ask us what had happened in the principal's office. We explained.

"I read that list you gave me this morning," Andrea said. "When Mrs. Dawson first told us about the circus I thought it sounded awesome, but now I don't want to go. Those circus people are mean."

"I'm taking that fact sheet home," Randy Furlan said. "My dad's a veterinarian. I'll show it to him and see what he thinks."

I felt better as I listened to my classmates. Instead of acting as if David and I were strange for not wanting to go to the circus, most of them were outraged by the cruelties that the Glitter Tent Circus had been charged with.

Maybe I'm not odd for caring so much, I thought. Maybe lots of kids love animals and, once they know about the abuse, they'll object as much as I do.

After we ate lunch we all went outside to play kickball, but David and I couldn't get interested in the game. We were too curious about the conversation between Mrs. Dawson and Dr. Martinez. Finally we left the play yard and went to the principal's office.

Through the open door we saw Dr. Martinez seated at his desk. When he saw us, he got up and came toward us.

"Mrs. Dawson decided not to change her plan," he said. "She believes a second field trip is unnecessary and would create conflict within the class. I will abide by her decision."

"What about all those animal cruelty cases?" I asked. "Did she ever read the fact sheet?"

"Mrs. Dawson says the issue is not animal cruelty; it's who is in charge of her class. She feels you are trying to undermine her authority."

"That isn't true," I said. "We just don't want to attend a circus that exploits animals."

"You are not to pass out your fact sheets or ask the other students to sign the petition," Dr. Martinez said.

"What if we do it when we're away from school?" I asked. "What if I have kids over to my house and we talk about the circus and they sign the petition?"

Dr. Martinez shook his head. "You are both excellent students," he said. "You've never been in trouble and this is your last month at Harborview Elementary. Don't risk a big black mark on your record now. My advice is to forget the petition. Even if everyone in your class signed it, which isn't likely, you can't force Mrs. Dawson to plan a different destination. She already has the tickets for the circus. She's arranged for a school bus for transportation, and she has a parent lined up to come along. She's gone to a lot of effort to plan this trip. No matter what you do, your class will be going to the circus. I suggest you go, too."

Tears filled my eyes and I blinked hard to keep them from spilling down my cheeks. It was so unfair. Just because Mrs. Dawson had been teaching here for a million years, Dr. Martinez was going to let her do what she wanted and there was nothing we could do about it.

"The circus will perform here in Harborview whether you go to it or not," Dr. Martinez said. "Then it will travel on to the next town and the one after that, for the whole summer. You can't change anything, so why cause a big fuss and get yourselves in trouble?"

"If we refuse to go, maybe other kids will refuse to go, too," I said. "If enough people stay away, the circus will go out of business."

"That is unlikely," he said.

The phone on his desk rang, and Dr. Martinez nodded at us to dismiss us.

As soon as we were out in the hall, I started to cry. I couldn't help it. This was so unfair!

"A local school censors its students," David said.

"Tune in at six to find out how two children were denied their right to speak the truth."

I wiped my eyes and struggled to get control of my emotions before we got back to class.

At afternoon recess we told the rest of the kids what had happened.

"I think you should do the petition, no matter what Dr. Martinez says," Pinkie said. "This is a free country. If we want to sign a petition, we can."

"That's right," Andrea said. "I haven't signed it yet, but I will. Where is it?"

I shook my head. "Dr. Martinez is right about the petition," I said. "It won't do any good even if the whole class signs it. If Mrs. Dawson wouldn't offer an alternate trip after Dr. Martinez suggested it, then she certainly won't do it because we fill up a petition—especially when we've been told *not* to do a petition."

"So what are you going to do?" Pinkie asked.

"We'll think of something," David said.

"I know one thing I won't do," I said. "I won't go to that circus."

"Neither will I," David said. "I'll skip school if I have to. I don't care if I get a black mark on my record."

Pinkie brightened. "If you're going to skip school," he said, "I'll skip with you."

Before school got out that afternoon, Mrs. Dawson passed out permission slips for the circus.

"Be sure to have a parent sign your slip," she said, "and bring it back tomorrow. I need to have these before you can leave the school."

I looked at David. I could tell he was thinking the same thing I was thinking: *What if we don't turn in our permission slips?*

As if she could read our minds, Mrs. Dawson said, "If anyone fails to return the slip by Thursday morning, that person's grade for the semester will be lowered one full point."

I've had an A average every semester since I started school. Lowering my grade by a full point would give me a B this time. Would that make a difference which classes I got next year? Would it mean I couldn't be in TAG?

Flora had told me I know too much. Maybe she's right, I thought, as I watched my classmates take the permission slips. If I didn't know so much about circus animals, I wouldn't care so much about the field trip. I thought of the old saying, *Ignorance is bliss,* and decided it was true.

When Mrs. Dawson got to our row, David and I each took one of the permission slips. I felt like tearing it into shreds and throwing it on the floor, but instead I stuck it into my backpack.

I decided to talk to Mom about this problem. Dad was out of town on business, but Mom would have some advice.

I didn't talk to her about it, though, because when

I got home Aunt Lorna and Misty were there, and Mom gave me terrible news.

"Nana's in the hospital," Mom said. "We need you to watch Misty until Kathleen gets home from soccer practice."

Nana is my grandmother. "What's wrong with her?" I asked.

"We don't know yet; the doctors are doing some tests now. She collapsed at a meeting of her quilting club, and her friends called nine-one-one. She may have had a heart attack."

I felt suddenly cold. How could Nana have a heart attack? She plays Michigan rummy with me and comes to my softball games and invites me to spend the night. I didn't want Nana to be in the hospital.

"We've been at the hospital since noon," Aunt Lorna said. "We left to pick up Misty from her preschool, and we're going back to the hospital now."

"You and Kathleen can fix dinner," Mom said, "and put Misty to bed here if we aren't back by eight o'clock."

I nodded. "We'll be fine," I said. "Tell Nana . . ." My lip quivered and my voice got shaky. "Tell Nana that I love her."

Mom hugged me. "I'll call when I learn anything," she said. Then she and Aunt Lorna were out the door.

5

Lilly Comes to Town

Misty and I colored pictures, then printed GET WELL, NANA on them. We went for a walk around the block, looking for four-leaf clovers. I stopped at David's house to tell him about Nana.

"Jason Jurrey called me," David said. Jason is in our class. "He agrees with us and doesn't want to go to the circus, either. He didn't say anything at school because he was afraid Mrs. Dawson would hear and get mad at him."

I wondered how many more of our classmates agreed with us but had said nothing.

At five-thirty, I put a frozen pizza in the oven. It was almost done when Kathleen got home. She cut up apples, pears, and bananas for a fruit salad.

We kept listening for the phone to ring, hoping Mom would call to tell us it was all a false alarm and that Nana was fine and they were taking her home.

We were cleaning up the kitchen when David came over. "Randy Furlan called," he said. "He showed our fact sheet to his dad and his dad told him the circus is arriving at the fairgrounds tonight. Dr. Furlan's supposed to go over there tomorrow morning because the elephant is limping."

"The circus actually called in a veterinarian?" I said. "They keep getting cited for *not* having veterinary care."

"Someone from the U.S. Department of Agriculture called Dr. Furlan. There were complaints about the elephant's condition in the last town where the circus performed, so they want the opinion of a veterinarian."

"Agriculture?" Kathleen said. "That would be farms, not a circus."

"The Department of Agriculture is supposed to enforce the Animal Welfare Act," I said.

"That's a national law to protect animals," David explained.

The phone rang. Kathleen beat me to it but I could tell it was Mom, with good news.

"Nana did have a heart attack," Kathleen said after she had hung up, "but it was mild. She needs to stay in the hospital for a couple of days for observation. Mom and Aunt Lorna are going to stay until ten, then Aunt Lorna will go back first thing tomorrow morning."

Kathleen and I grinned at each other. Nana was out of danger.

"Since you know your grandma's okay, do you want to walk over to the fairgrounds with me to watch the circus arrive?" David asked. "Maybe we can see them unload the animals."

"When are you going?" I asked.

"Now. Dr. Furlan thought they would get here soon."

I looked at Kathleen.

"It's okay with me," she said. "You took care of Misty while I was at soccer practice. I can put her to bed."

"Thanks," I said.

"It'll cost you when you get home," Kathleen said. "I need a slogan for Petal Pink's new peppermint-scented toilet tissue."

"Peppermint-scented?" David said. "You have to be kidding."

"Their idea is that the bathroom will have this fresh peppermint smell," Kathleen said.

"No more stink with Petal Pink," I said.

David laughed.

"That's perfect!" Kathleen said. She grabbed a scrap of paper and wrote down the slogan.

Misty giggled and began to chant, "No stink. No stink."

"What's the prize?" I asked.

"Five years' supply of Petal Pink peppermint-scented toilet tissue," Kathleen said.

"I can hardly wait," I said as I grabbed a sweatshirt and headed toward the door with David.

"Be home before dark or Mom will have a fit," Kathleen said.

"What are you going to do about the permission slip for the circus?" David asked as we walked the mile to the fairgrounds. "I don't want to have my grade cut."

"I had an idea," I said. "Let's get our slips signed and turn them in, as if we were planning to go to the circus. Then on Thursday when it's time to go, we'll sit at our desks."

"We'll refuse to board the bus?"

"That's right. We'll politely say we prefer to stay in school, then remain seated. What is Mrs. Dawson going to do—drag us out of our seats and carry us to the bus?"

"It will be a sit-in," David said, "like they had for civil rights. How can we be punished for staying in school?"

"We can tell the kids who signed our petition what we plan to do. Maybe they'll stay at school with us."

David's eyes sparkled. "If we turn in the permission slips, Mrs. Dawson will assume that we're going. By the time she finds out we aren't, it will be time for the bus to leave. Any kids who want to go to the circus can do so; the rest of us will stay in class."

"I wonder if any of the other kids will do this."

"Erin, look!" David pointed. "There they are."

A long line of big trucks and trailers drove through the fairgrounds entrance, then circled around toward the back of the arena. All had a logo on the side showing a tiger, an elephant, and a horse. Bright gold letters said GLITTER TENT CIRCUS.

"Let's watch them unload," David said. "Maybe we can see the animals. If the people are mean to them, we'll call the police or Dr. Furlan."

"If they hurt the animals, I don't want to look."

"I wish we'd brought a camera," David said. He switched to his deep voice. "A future news broadcaster snapped a photo today that's being shown on television around the world."

As we approached the open gate where the circus trucks were entering, a man shouted at us. "Hey, you kids! Get out of here! The circus doesn't open until tomorrow."

"We're looking for a lost cat," David said. "We think he's inside the fence."

"Go home!" the man yelled. "Nobody's allowed in here except circus employees."

David and I retreated. We did not go home, however. We walked along the outside of the chain link fence where we could see what happened inside the fairgrounds.

The man who had yelled at us directed the trucks where to park. He called instructions to a group of men who began driving stakes into the ground and hauling huge canvas tents out of two trailers. He was as surly with the men as he had been with David and me.

"Where are the animals?" I said. "Shouldn't they unload the animals first? They've been confined in those trailers while they were driven here."

Near where the circus trucks were parked we saw a man and woman with clipboards observing the circus setup through the fence. They looked as if they were about twenty years old.

"What if they wait until dark before they unload the animals?" the man said as we approached. "We won't be able to see."

"Let's go around to the gate," the woman replied. "Maybe they'll let us in."

David said, "They wouldn't let us in."

The couple turned to us. "Hi," she said. "Are you with an animal welfare group, too?"

"No," I said. "We're just curious to see how the circus animals are treated."

"I'm Nancy and this is Mike," she said. "We're with a group called STAC—Stop Animal Cruelty—that is investigating the Glitter Tent Circus."

"We're in big trouble with our teacher because we don't want to go to the circus with our class," David said.

"Oh?" said Nancy.

"What kind of trouble?" asked Mike. "Tell us about it."

We explained about the field trip and how Mrs. Dawson would not offer an alternate trip and how our principal was backing her in her decision.

"Is it okay with you if we tell a reporter about this?" Nancy asked. "One of the Harborview television stations plans to do a special story on the circus, and they're looking for local angles."

"Sure," I said. "Our whole school knows about it, so it isn't any secret."

Nancy wrote down my name and David's name, and which school we attend.

Two circus workers approached one of the large trailers. They opened it and one climbed inside. Soon a ramp thudded down to the ground, providing a walkway from the trailer.

"Get out now! Move along!" The shouts came from inside the trailer.

Beside me Nancy whispered, "Start the camera."

Mike raised a small video camera and pointed it toward the ramp.

An elephant emerged from the trailer. Chains dangled from her right front ankle and her left rear ankle. Two men on the ground put metal bars through the chains. The elephant stopped when she was partway down the ramp.

"Move it!" yelled the man inside. He jumped

down and stood in front of the elephant, holding a long stick with a sharp hook on the end.

Beside me I heard the video camera whirring.

"Get down here, Lilly!" the man shouted. "We don't have all night."

The elephant swayed back and forth but did not move forward. The man thrust the stick toward the elephant and hooked the sharp end into the skin behind one front knee. When he yanked on the stick, the elephant jerked that leg forward, causing the chain to clang against the metal ramp.

The man put the hook behind the elephant's other front knee and jerked again. "Move it, Lilly!" he shouted.

I cringed, imagining how painful that sharp hook would be in the tender skin at the back of the knee.

Lilly plodded forward and stepped off the ramp.

The two men holding the chains quickly attached them to steel posts that had been driven into the ground. I realized that Lilly could not move around at all, chained the way she was. She couldn't even lie down.

Mike continued to film the elephant, talking quietly so that his voice was on the video but not heard by the circus trainers. "Elephants in the wild," Mike said, "often walk thirty miles per day. They are social animals, who stay in family groups all their lives. Lilly, the circus elephant, spends ninety-nine percent of her time in chains, alone."

The two circus workers walked away from Lilly toward the next trailer. They had not given her water or anything to eat.

As they left, Lilly turned her head toward us and for an instant I looked directly into her eyes. She seemed incredibly sad.

I pressed my face into the chain link fence. "Oh, Lilly," I whispered. "You should not have to live this way."

Nancy put a hand on my shoulder.

"I wish I could help Lilly," I said.

"You are helping her," Nancy said. "Refusing to attend the circus is the most important thing you can do for her."

"It's almost dark," David said. "We'd better leave."

I thought about Lilly all the way home.

I kept expecting David to say one of his pretend news headlines about the elephant, but he didn't.

6

The TV Interview

I couldn't stop thinking about Lilly—about the chains and the hook that was used to make her move, and about her unhappy, lonely life. No animal should have such a wretched existence.

Nancy had said that by refusing to attend the circus I was doing the best I could to help the elephant, but I wished I could do more.

On the way to school the next morning I told David, "We need to be careful who we talk to. We should tell our sit-in plan only to kids who approach us and say they don't want to go to the circus. The plan won't work if Mrs. Dawson knows in advance what we're going to do, because then she'll have time to think of a way to make us go. She has to be surprised."

"Don't tell Flora," David said.

"Ha! No way."

"How's your grandma?"

"Better. Aunt Lorna's at the hospital today, then Mom will go when she gets off work."

"Did you get your permission slip signed?"

"Yes, but I didn't have a chance to talk to Mom about what we're doing. I left the slip on the table last night and when I got up this morning it was signed. There was a note from Mom. She went in to work early so she can go to the hospital in time for Aunt Lorna to pick up Misty."

"I got mine signed, too," David said.

"I feel odd planning to disobey Mrs. Dawson," I said. "I've never been in trouble with a teacher before."

"She's being unreasonable."

"Still, I wish we could have solved this another way. Except for being boring, Mrs. Dawson is an okay teacher and I don't like to make her angry."

Randy, Jason, Andrea, and Scooter met us in front of the school.

"We don't want to go to the circus," Scooter said.

"My dad says I don't have to go," Randy said.

"My mom says you should sue the school for not letting you get your petition signed," Andrea said.

"I didn't get my permission slip signed," Jason said.

I told them about the sit-in.

"I'll stay in school with you," Jason said.

"So will I," Andrea said.

"I'll do a sit-in for the elephant," Scooter said.

"Get your permission slips signed and turn them in tomorrow," I said. "That way Mrs. Dawson won't be suspicious."

"Be careful who you tell," David warned.

The others nodded.

"Judy and Greg told me they looked at that web site about circuses that you told us about," Andrea said. "They want a different field trip, too."

Scooter said, "Chelsea said she was happy when Mrs. Dawson told us we were going to the circus, but after she read your fact sheet she changed her mind."

"If anyone tells you they don't want to go," I said, "let them know our plan."

Mrs. Dawson looked surprised when David and I handed in our permission slips but she didn't say anything. She reminded those who had not brought their slips back to be sure to do so the next day.

During morning recess a white van with TV call letters on the side parked next to the playground. A cameraman got out and took a shot of the sign that says HARBORVIEW ELEMENTARY SCHOOL.

All the kids quit playing and watched as the cameraman and a woman carrying a black case came up the walkway. I recognized the woman; it was Jill Gentile, who does the five o'clock news.

Mrs. Lorel went over to Jill and said, "May I help you?"

"We'd like to speak with the teacher who's taking her class to the circus," Jill said, "and to Erin Wrenn and David Showers, the children who don't want to go."

"You'll need to go to the office first," Mrs. Lorel said. "All visitors are required to sign in there. Ask for Dr. Martinez, the principal."

"Thanks," Jill said.

The news traveled through the student body like a lightning bolt. Within seconds, every kid in Harborview School knew that two people from a TV station were there to see David and me. I didn't even want to think about what Mrs. Dawson would say.

When recess ended, we rushed back to our room. Dr. Martinez met us in the hall, looking annoyed, and told us we would need to wait quietly for a few minutes. Through the open door, I saw Jill Gentile talking to Mrs. Dawson while the cameraman filmed the conversation.

My whole class crowded around the door, straining to see and hear.

"I understand you refused to offer your class an alternate field trip, after some of the students objected to the circus," Jill said.

"There is no need for a second field trip," Mrs. Dawson said. "Only two students complained about the circus. All the rest are thrilled to be going."

"Are you aware of the cruelty charges filed against Glitter Tent Circus?" Jill asked.

"I've seen a few allegations that were posted on a web site," Mrs. Dawson said, "but there is a great deal of misinformation on the Internet."

Jill said, "What do you think your students will learn from attending the circus tomorrow?"

"They'll learn how exciting live entertainment is," Mrs. Dawson said. "They've seen tigers and elephants on film, but to see them perform in person is entirely different." For the first time since the interview began, Mrs. Dawson smiled. "I am giving my students a happy, memorable day—the kind of day my grandfather gave me every summer when he took me to the circus. It will be a wonderful, educational experience."

"The circus manager refused to let us on the fairgrounds this morning while a veterinarian examined an elephant," Jill said.

Out in the hall, Randy whispered, "That was my dad!"

Jill continued, "Two local groups are currently investigating this circus. If proof of cruelty is found, would that change your mind about taking your class to the circus?"

"My students are waiting to return to class," Mrs. Dawson said. "I think I'd better end this discussion."

I almost felt sorry for her. It seemed obvious that

she was going to believe what she wanted to believe, regardless of the facts. I didn't blame her for wanting to hold on to her happy memories of her grandfather; since yesterday I had thought a lot about Nana, and the things we've done together.

Why couldn't Mrs. Dawson keep her happy memories and, at the same time, acknowledge that this circus mistreats its animals and isn't a good place for a field trip?

Jill Gentile thanked Mrs. Dawson for talking to her.

Dr. Martinez said, "Erin and David, please stay in the hall. The rest of you may go in now and take your seats."

"Are Erin and David going to be interviewed?" Jason asked. "Will they be on TV?"

"Maybe," Dr. Martinez said.

"I want to watch," Jason said.

As Dr. Martinez was ushering Jason through the door, Jill Gentile and the cameraman came into the hall.

Scooter immediately went over to Jill and whispered something to her. "Oh?" she said.

"Scooter!" Dr. Martinez said. "Take your seat."

Scooter went to his desk.

As soon as the other students were in the room, Dr. Martinez closed the classroom door. Then he said, "Erin and David, these folks would like to ask you a few questions."

"How did you get interested in the plight of circus animals?" Jill asked.

David explained about our TAG project.

"I understand you handed out information about the Glitter Tent Circus at school yesterday."

"We did until Mrs. Dawson and Dr. Martinez made us stop," I said.

"What did your classmates say about your information?"

"Some of them don't want to go to the circus now," David said.

"How do you feel about attending the circus tomorrow?"

"I don't want to go," I said. "If we ignore this cruelty, it will continue to happen. The best way to stop it is to stay away from the circus. Circuses will stop using animals only when people quit paying to see those animals."

"There are circuses that have only people performing, not animals," David said. "If everyone would support those circuses, then the ones that use tigers and elephants and bears would quit using the animals."

"We went to the fairgrounds last night," I said. "We saw an elephant named Lilly. Her feet were chained so she could barely move. She looked so sad that it made me cry."

"Thank you both for sharing your thoughts," Jill said, as she signaled the photographer to quit filming.

"You may go back to class," Dr. Martinez said. "Try not to disrupt the lesson."

David and I slipped into our seats, while the rest of the class stared at us. Mrs. Dawson kept talking about long division, as if nothing unusual had happened.

At lunch David and I were celebrities. The others wanted to know what had been said, and they all vowed to watch the five o'clock news that evening.

Kathleen, David, and I watched the broadcast together. The Glitter Tent Circus was the lead story. The news anchorman said, "There's a controversy in Harborview this week, because the circus is in town. A local teacher is on one side of the issue, but some of her students disagree. Jill Gentile has the story."

The screen showed the Harborview School sign, then Jill explained the problem. They showed the interview with Mrs. Dawson, followed by David and me. A few things had been cut out, and I wished I had combed my hair.

After I told how we saw Lilly in chains, the report switched to Dr. Furlan, Randy's dad.

"The elephant has some foot rot," Dr. Furlan said, "and her toenails have chips and cracks. It is difficult for her to walk. There are puncture wounds behind her ears, behind her knees, and under her chin where the trainers have used a bullhook. Three of those wounds are badly infected. Lilly is only fifteen years old but she moves more like an elderly animal. She is seriously underweight, and there are no veterinary records for her."

Beside me on the couch, Kathleen said, "This wouldn't happen if you were president."

"Shh," I said.

Next, Jill Gentile spoke with a man named Harold Hinkley, who was the manager of the circus. I recognized him as the one who had chased us away from the fairgrounds gate.

"I'm used to false accusations from well-meaning but misguided animal lovers," Mr. Hinkley said. "All the animals in the Glitter Tent Circus are well cared for."

"What about the infected wounds on Lilly?" Jill asked.

"We may have overlooked those," Mr. Hinkley admitted. "The truth is, Lilly is no longer able to perform all of her tricks so we plan to sell her soon."

"To whom?" Jill asked. "Who buys elephants?"

"Our animals usually go to Big Game, Incorporated."

The picture switched from Mr. Hinkley to Mike and Nancy, the people David and I had met at the fairgrounds.

"The Animal Welfare Act is a law to protect animals," Mike said. "It requires that all confined animals have enough room to stand up and turn around, but even that basic law has routinely been broken by this circus."

Nancy told about some of the worst citations received by Glitter Tent Circus.

Jill said, "The circus owner tells us that his elephant will be sold soon to Big Game, Incorporated. Reporter Kevin St. John has some information about that company."

"It's a big hunting reserve," the reporter said. "They buy old or sick animals from private zoos and circuses, then turn them loose on a fenced ranch. Hunters pay thousands of dollars for the chance to shoot an animal and take its head as a trophy. Trophy hunting reserves are a very lucrative business."

The news switched to commercials, and Kathleen turned off the sound.

I felt sick to my stomach. Lilly was finally going to be free of her chains, only to get murdered by a hunter.

7

The Sixth-grade Sit-in

Within seconds after our part of the news broadcast ended, Mom called; she and Nana had watched the news at the hospital. Andrea called to say her mom had taped the broadcast and she would bring me a copy tomorrow.

Scooter called next. "I told that reporter that she should come back to school tomorrow," he said, "when the class is scheduled to go to the circus."

"Did you tell her what we're going to do?"

"Nope. I said the story wasn't over yet and she should show up at eleven tomorrow morning."

"Thanks for warning me," I said.

When I told David about Scooter's call, he said, "Police were summoned to Harborview Elementary School today after a teacher had a conniption in front of her students."

"Mrs. Dawson won't be pleased," I agreed, "and neither will Dr. Martinez. On the other hand, the more publicity we get, the more likely it is that other people will stay away from the circus."

"Wouldn't it be great," David said, "if the whole class refused to go? We'd be on the news again for sure."

"Flora will go," I said, "and Pinkie would never stay in school voluntarily."

The phone kept ringing as classmates called to discuss the newscast.

Randy told us that three other parents had called his dad after seeing the news broadcast and said their kids don't want to go to the circus now. Judy said she had talked about the circus at her gymnastics workout and two other girls from our class, Winnie and Michelle, had decided to join the sit-in. Jason had talked to Bob, and Bob had talked to Linda. They planned to stay in school.

Each phone call made me more excited—and more nervous—about our plan for the next day. When the calls finally stopped, David and I wrote down the names of all the kids who had said they wanted to stay in school rather than go to the circus.

If all the kids who said they were going to refuse to go to the circus actually followed through, there would be eighteen of us in our seats and only ten getting on the bus.

I hardly slept that night. My biggest fear was that, with so many people knowing about the sit-in, the plan would accidentally get back to Mrs. Dawson or Dr. Martinez. I believed I was doing the right thing, but I also knew my teacher and principal would not approve, and I wasn't sure what would happen if they found out ahead of time.

When David and I got to school the next morning, we were the center of attention. Even kids we didn't know stopped us to say, "I saw you on TV last night." Some classmates whispered, "I heard about the sit-in. I'm staying here with you."

After the morning announcements, Mrs. Dawson used her kindergarten voice to say, "The day we've all been waiting for is finally here. I'm happy to say that all of you have turned in your permission slips, and we'll be leaving for the circus promptly at eleven o'clock."

Pinkie poked me in the back. "Are you really going?" he whispered. "I didn't think you'd back down."

I did not answer him.

"Dr. Martinez and Mrs. Gummer will be going, too," Mrs. Dawson said. "I trust you will all use your best manners."

Flora said, "I wore my new dress today."

David rolled his eyes as if to say, "Whoopee for you."

In a way, I envied Flora. It would be simpler to go

to the circus than to remain in school. While Flora was cheering for the tiger when it jumped through fire, and clapping for the elephant's tricks, I would be fretting about the consequences of the sit-in.

Yet I knew I had to stay in my seat when the time came. If I didn't, I would go against my own deepest beliefs about what was right. Once I knew about the mistreated animals, I could not ignore those facts.

The clock seemed to move more slowly than usual as I worried about what would happen at eleven o'clock. Would the other kids have the courage to stay in their seats with Dr. Martinez looking at them? Would David and I be the only ones who didn't go? Would we get kicked out of school for not going to the circus? Would the TV crew come again? I fidgeted through a spelling test and long division without even knowing what I was doing.

At ten minutes to eleven, Mrs. Gummer arrived. A few minutes later Dr. Martinez came in and said, "The bus driver called. He'll be here shortly."

Right after that, Jill Gentile and the photographer came to our classroom door.

"All right!" Scooter said.

I glanced at David. He looked as uneasy as I felt.

"We'd like to get a shot of the class leaving for the circus," Jill said. "Sort of a follow-up to yesterday's broadcast. Is that okay?"

"It doesn't seem very newsworthy," Dr. Martinez

said, "but I have no objection." He turned to Mrs. Dawson. "Let's go," he said.

Mrs. Dawson said, "Class, our big moment has arrived. I want you to stand quietly and walk out to the bus. Mrs. Gummer and Flora will go first; the rest of you may follow by rows."

Flora stood and strutted to the front of the room. I heard the video camera start filming. Five other kids, including Pinkie, got up and followed Flora. The rest of us stayed in our seats.

Mrs. Gummer and Flora stopped at the door and waited.

Mrs. Dawson looked confused. She repeated her instructions. Twenty-two kids remained in their seats.

"I want everyone—*everyone*—on that bus," she said, "including you, Erin, and you, David. Right now!"

"I'm sorry, Mrs. Dawson," I said, "but I am not going to the circus. I choose to stay in school."

"I'm not going, either," David said.

Other voices joined in.

"I don't like this circus."

"I'd rather stay here than support people who are mean to animals."

"My dad said I don't have to go."

"If you did not plan to go," Mrs. Dawson said, "why did you turn in your signed permission slips?"

"Because you said you would lower my grade by a

full point if I didn't turn in the slip," David said.

At that, Dr. Martinez made a choking sound. He said, "Anyone who wishes to skip the circus and remain in school may do so."

"But the bus will be nearly empty," Mrs. Dawson said, "and I have all those free tickets. We can't leave the class unattended. We'll need to find a substitute, and there's not time."

"I'll stay here," Dr. Martinez said. "With so few children going, you don't need me to chaperon."

Mrs. Dawson looked as if she were about to cry. She turned to me and said, "Our happy day is spoiled. You let your personal feelings ruin the reward that the whole class earned."

She turned and marched out of the classroom. Mrs. Gummer and Flora followed her. So did four of the kids who had stood up. The last one in line, Pinkie, hesitated at the door, then returned to his seat.

"I never thought I would stay in school if I didn't have to," Pinkie said, "but you are right about this, and Mrs. Dawson is wrong."

When Pinkie plopped down at his desk, I felt like cheering.

8

Erin's Idea

The cameraman stopped filming.

Dr. Martinez spoke to Jill Gentile. "I hope you won't blow this incident out of proportion," he said. "Mrs. Dawson is a dedicated teacher and even though she may not have handled this situation as well as she might have, her intentions were good and I don't want her to be embarrassed. The truth is, if I had this to do over I would handle it differently myself."

When the TV people had left, Dr. Martinez said, "Well, you certainly pulled off a surprise."

Nobody spoke.

I expected him to lecture us or tell us we had to spend the afternoon scrubbing gum off the bottoms of the cafeteria tables, but he didn't.

He called the school secretary on the intercom

and said, "Please contact Mrs. Mapes. Tell her we're canceling the second-grade TAG class today and ask her to cover Mrs. Dawson's students for the rest of the day."

When Mrs. Mapes arrived, Dr. Martinez told her what had happened, then left.

Mrs. Mapes said, "Whose idea was this?"

"Mine," I said.

"I thought so."

"We all wanted to do it," Andrea said.

"How do you feel about it now?" Mrs. Mapes asked.

"I'm astonished," Pinkie said. "I still can't believe I stayed in school by choice."

Mrs. Mapes looked at me. "Erin," she said. "How do you feel?"

"I'm glad we refused to go," I said, "but I wish I could do more for the elephant that I saw. Even if the Glitter Tent Circus closes from lack of attendance, Lilly will still get sold to the hunting ranch."

"Why do they have to sell her to a place like that," David said, "just so some guy can feel all macho by shooting her? Why couldn't they send her to that sanctuary we read about?"

"What sanctuary?" Mrs. Mapes asked.

"It's a place that takes needy or sick elephants and lets them live out their lives in natural surroundings," David said. "I think it's in Tennessee."

"That's it!" I shouted. The skin on my arms

prickled with excitement. "We'll send Lilly to the elephant sanctuary!"

"How are you going to talk Mr. Hinkley into giving his elephant to a sanctuary instead of selling her to the hunting ranch?" David said. "He doesn't seem the type to pass up a chance for some profit."

"He doesn't have to," I said. "We'll buy Lilly."

There were a few seconds of silence when my words hung in the air.

"Us?" David said.

"Yes, us," I said, looking around at my classmates. "All of us together. Let's call the circus, find out how much they want for Lilly, and then raise the money."

I could almost feel the electricity in the room as the other kids considered my idea.

"I'll help raise money," Pinkie said. "I'm good at mowing grass."

"I'll baby-sit," Judy said.

"I'll ask my grandma to donate," Andrea said. "She's always giving money to groups that help animals, and I walk her dog every day after school, for free."

Ideas rose all around me, like soap bubbles from a blower.

"We could have a car wash."

"Let's do a bake sale."

"We'll put on a talent show."

"Before you get too excited," Mrs. Mapes said,

"you need to make certain that it is possible to purchase Lilly and send her to the sanctuary. What do you think you should do first?"

"We should call the sanctuary," David said, "and find out if they have space for another elephant. This plan will work only if they'll take Lilly. We don't have any way to care for her."

"We can look up the sanctuary on the Internet, and get their phone number," I said. "If Dr. Martinez will let us make a long distance call, we can contact them right now."

"I have a cell phone in my purse," Mrs. Mapes said. "Let's go to the library and find your sanctuary on the computer."

We did a search for "elephant sanctuary" and there it was. We got the site on three of the library's computers, so everyone could see.

We looked at photos of elephants wandering freely on eight hundred acres of land that includes spring-fed ponds for drinking water, and wild bamboo, a favorite elephant treat. The sanctuary has only one purpose: to provide a place where sick, old, or needy elephants can walk the earth in peace and dignity.

I thought of Lilly with her infected sores and her legs in chains. *Please have room for her,* I thought. *Please, please say you'll take Lilly.*

We printed out some of the information, including the page that had the sanctuary's address and telephone number, and took it back to our classroom.

"Will you call the sanctuary for us?" I asked Mrs. Mapes. "An adult will be taken more seriously than a child."

She dialed the number and we all listened as she explained that she was calling for a group of sixth-grade students who wanted to purchase a circus elephant and send her to the sanctuary.

She listened for a moment, then said, "Let me ask." She turned to me and said, "The sanctuary is only for Asian elephants, because African elephants eat trees and are more aggressive. Is Lilly an Asian elephant?"

"I don't know," I said.

Mrs. Mapes told the sanctuary that she would find out. Then she said, "Of course. That's understandable. She was checked by a local veterinarian a few days ago. Perhaps he could call you." She listened, making notes.

"What about transportation?" she asked. "If my students are able to raise the money to buy Lilly, how do we get her to you?"

Mrs. Mapes made more notes, then gave her name, address, and phone number before she said, "Thank you. I'll have Dr. Furlan call you, and I'll let you know what arrangements we make with the circus."

She hung up, smiling at us. "Most circus elephants are Asian elephants," she said. "If that's what Lilly is and if we document that she is being mistreated, the sanctuary will accept her. They'll even send a custom-built elephant transport trailer and an experienced animal handler to drive her there."

"Who pays for all that?" Scooter asked.

"Private donors. The elephant sanctuary is a non-profit organization, funded by individuals who care about animals."

"Cool," said Scooter. "If I ever get rich, I'm going to give money to places like that."

"What's your next move?" Mrs. Mapes asked the class.

"Contact Mr. Hinkley," I said, "and find out what kind of elephant Lilly is and how much money he wants for her."

"What if Mr. Hinkley won't sell her?" Andrea said.

"He'll sell," Mrs. Mapes said. "It's just a question of price."

"What if he wants a million dollars?" Pinkie said.

"Then you'll have to mow a lot of grass," I said, "because we're going to do this. We're going to save Lilly!"

9

Big Plans

When Mrs. Mapes tried to call Mr. Hinkley she got an answering machine. She left her name and phone number but didn't say what she wanted.

Randy called his dad at the veterinary clinic, and told him what we wanted to do. "Do you know if Lilly is an Asian elephant?" he asked. Then he nodded and gave the thumbs-up sign to the rest of us as he told his dad the phone number of the elephant sanctuary.

"Dad says he's positive Lilly's an Asian elephant," Randy said after he hung up, "because she has five nails on her forefeet and four nails on her hindfeet. African elephants have one less nail on each foot. Also, Asian elephants have smaller ears."

I remembered that Dr. Furlan had talked on the TV news about the condition of Lilly's nails.

Randy continued, "Dad will call the sanctuary right now to discuss Lilly's condition. He also said he'll donate his time and the medication to treat Lilly's infected wounds before she leaves."

"All right!" David said, and we all took turns giving Randy high-fives.

"Is there anyone else you need to discuss this plan with?" Mrs. Mapes asked.

"We should tell our parents," I said. "We'll need their support. We could call Nancy and Mike, the people from STAC who were on the news. Maybe their group will help us raise the money."

Mrs. Mapes nodded her approval. "Who else?" she asked.

"Dr. Martinez," David said. "If this is going to be a class project, we should be sure it's okay with him."

Mrs. Mapes asked Dr. Martinez to come into the room for a few minutes. When he arrived, she said, "Erin, please tell Dr. Martinez your idea and what this class hopes to do."

I stood. I told him about the elephant sanctuary and about our plan to raise the money to buy Lilly and send her there. When I finished, Mrs. Mapes showed Dr. Martinez the information we had printed, and asked him to read more about the elephant sanctuary on their web site.

I crossed my fingers, knowing that we needed Dr. Martinez's approval if we had any hope of succeeding.

Dr. Martinez looked at us with a surprised expression, as if he had never seen any of us before. "So you're going to buy an elephant," he said.

"Yes, sir," I said. The rest of the kids nodded their heads yes.

"Well, I must say I'm proud of you," Dr. Martinez said. "Most people complain when something is wrong but they don't take any action to correct the problem."

Relief washed over me. Dr. Martinez was on our side.

"This won't be easy," he warned. "I expect the price will be several thousand dollars."

"We don't care," Andrea said. "We're going to have a car wash and a bake sale, and we'll all donate our money from pulling weeds and baby-sitting and whatever other jobs we can get."

"We're going to save Lilly," I said.

Dr. Martinez smiled at me. "Yes," he said, "I believe you are."

The recess bell rang but none of us wanted to go outside. We were afraid Mr. Hinkley would call and we didn't want to miss that.

Mrs. Mapes said we needed to go out and work off some of our energy but she let Judy stay inside to act as a runner. If the phone call came, Judy would rush out to let the rest of us know.

Some of the class played kickball but most of us stood around talking about Lilly.

"I wish we could help all the circus animals," I said. "Mr. Hinkley has tigers and lions and horses who are mistreated, too."

"We did help all of them by not going to the circus and by getting lots of publicity," David said.

"I want to save them all," I said, even though I knew that wasn't possible.

"Maybe after we rescue the elephant, other people will want to rescue an animal, too," Andrea said.

I hoped she was right. Realistically, I knew I couldn't save every needy circus animal any more than I could adopt every dog and cat at the Harborview animal shelter. When I chose Beanie from the shelter, it broke my heart to leave the other homeless dogs and cats behind, but Mom and Dad insisted that one pet was enough.

One animal at a time, I told myself. I gave Beanie a loving home and now I am going to save Lilly and send her to the sanctuary. I will do the best I can for one animal at a time.

When recess ended, we went back inside. We were discussing possible dates for fund-raising events, when Mr. Hinkley called.

The room was as quiet as a deserted library as each of us listened to one side of the conversation and tried to guess the other side.

"Thank you, Mr. Hinkley," Mrs. Mapes said at last. "I'll see you on Saturday."

She closed the phone. "He wouldn't name a price

over the phone," she said, "but he's willing to talk about it in person. I'm going to meet with him at ten o'clock Saturday morning."

"Couldn't he meet you tonight or tomorrow?" I said. "I can't wait until Saturday."

"Saturday morning was most convenient for him," Mrs. Mapes said. "If I pushed for an earlier time, I would seem too eager and he might raise the price."

"May we go with you?" Andrea asked.

"It would be best if you elect one student to represent all of you. He or she can go with me. It might be wise to invite Dr. Martinez to go, too."

"I think we should send Erin," Greg said. "Saving Lilly was her idea. She's the one who thought of staying in school today as a way to protest the circus, and she's the one who suggested we buy Lilly and move her to the sanctuary."

The vote was unanimous.

I was glad to be chosen but at the same time it made me nervous. Mr. Hinkley did not seem to be a pleasant man.

I was relieved when Dr. Martinez agreed to go along. With him and Mrs. Mapes there, maybe I wouldn't actually have to say anything.

"There's one more person you need to tell about this plan," Mrs. Mapes said.

I glanced at David. We both knew who Mrs. Mapes meant.

"We need to tell Mrs. Dawson," I said.

"Why?" asked Pinkie. "She won't help us. She thinks Lilly is living a life of luxury."

"If you want to work together as a class," Mrs. Mapes said, "you'll need Mrs. Dawson's help. You should try to involve the whole class, if possible, including those students who chose to attend the circus today."

"What if Mrs. Dawson won't let us work on raising money for Lilly during school hours?" Andrea said.

"Then we'll do it after school," I said, "but it would be a lot easier if we could talk about it here, when we're all together."

"The bus may get back to school before we leave," Mrs. Mapes said. "If not, you should call Mrs. Dawson at home this evening, Erin, and tell her what you've decided to do."

My stomach turned a backflip at the thought of calling Mrs. Dawson. She would probably hang up on me. She might already be so angry that she'd have me transferred out of her class. Maybe she'd never speak to me again.

"It would be better for her to hear about this from you right at the beginning," Mrs. Mapes said, "than to suspect that you are doing it behind her back."

"If Mrs. Dawson helps us do this," I said, "she will be admitting that the circus people have mistreated Lilly. That won't be easy for her."

"No, it won't," Mrs. Mapes said, "and she may

not be willing to do it, but you must offer her the chance to help you."

Reluctantly, I agreed to tell Mrs. Dawson that while she and five of her students were at the circus watching the elephant perform, the rest of her sixth-grade class decided to buy that elephant and send her to a better life.

The field trip bus did not get back to school by dismissal time, so Mrs. Mapes gave me Mrs. Dawson's home number. I dreaded the call. I wished I could have Mrs. Mapes and Dr. Martinez to back me up when I talked to her, but I knew I couldn't. I had to talk to Mrs. Dawson by myself.

10

Face-to-Face with Mrs. Dawson

At five o'clock that afternoon, David pounded on the door.

"Turn on your TV," he yelled. "They're going to show the follow-up story about our class refusing to go to the circus."

I was so nervous about calling Mrs. Dawson, I had forgotten about the news. Kathleen was watching a talk show but she heard David and switched channels.

As soon as the commercials finished, Jill Gentile came on. She told about our field trip and then ran the tape of me and David and the others telling Mrs. Dawson we wanted to stay in school.

"In the end," Jill said, "only five of the twenty-eight students in this class went to the circus today."

She didn't run any footage of Mrs. Dawson.

Instead she switched to another interview with Nancy, the woman from STAC.

"The district attorney filed an animal cruelty charge against Glitter Tent Circus today," Nancy said. "One of our members got a temporary job at the circus, and he took video of an animal trainer beating the elephant."

When they showed the video, I closed my eyes, feeling sick. Poor Lilly.

"Is that the elephant you're going to buy?" Kathleen asked.

"Yes," I said.

"I'll help," Kathleen said. "You can have my allowance and all my baby-sitting money. I have twenty dollars saved for a new swimsuit but I can wear my old one."

"Thanks," I said.

"I wonder if Mrs. Dawson saw this newscast," David said.

I didn't want to think about Mrs. Dawson.

When I finally got up my courage and dialed her number, I got an answering machine.

I hung up and tried later. I got the machine again. That time I left a message: "Hi, Mrs. Dawson. This is Erin Wrenn. I need to talk to you before school tomorrow. If you get this message before ten o'clock tonight, please call me at 555-2398. Otherwise I'll come to school half an hour early and hope to see you then."

If it would be hard to talk to Mrs. Dawson on the phone, it would be even harder to meet with her in person, but I couldn't think what else to do.

I waited until ten-fifteen for her call; then I gave up and went to bed.

Mom got home soon after I turned out my light. She peeked in my room. "Are you awake?" she whispered.

"Yes."

"I have good news. Nana's feeling much better. She'll probably come home from the hospital on Saturday."

"Good," I said. I shifted position to make Beanie get off my legs. He loves to sleep stretched out on top of me.

"Nana and I saw your sit-in on the news," Mom said. "I'm sorry I haven't been home this week to talk with you about the circus."

"My class is going to buy the elephant," I said, "and send her to a sanctuary."

"What?"

Mom sat on the edge of my bed and heard the whole story. When I finished, she said, "You've been crazy about animals ever since you could walk, but I never thought you'd buy an elephant." She kissed me good night. "I can't wait to tell your father."

Feeling better, I petted Beanie and fell asleep listening to him purr.

David called early the next morning.

"What did Mrs. Dawson say?" he asked.

"I couldn't reach her. I left a message but she didn't call back so I'm going to school early to talk to her."

"Do you want me to come with you?"

"Yes," I said, grateful to have such a loyal friend. "I'm leaving now; I'm too nervous to eat breakfast."

David met me out in front, munching a bagel and cream cheese.

"I told my dad about Lilly," he said. "Dad says if Mr. Hinkley is unreasonable at your meeting tomorrow, you should say that Dad is your attorney and he is following the animal cruelty case with great interest."

David finished the bagel, wiped his hands on his jeans, and dug a business card out of his pocket. "Dad says people like that get nervous when they hear the word *attorney.* Here's one of his business cards, in case you need it."

I took the card.

Mrs. Gummer dropped Flora off as David and I arrived at school.

"Do you suppose she comes early every day?" David asked.

When Flora saw us, she followed us inside. "You really missed a fun day," she said. "The circus was fantastic. You guys were so stupid to stay at school."

I pressed my lips together, determined not to quarrel with Flora.

"Did you see us on the news last night?" David said.

"No," Flora said. "Did it show me?"

"They showed the kids who stayed at school," I said.

"Oh," Flora said. "How come you're here so early today?"

"Why are *you* here so early?" I countered.

"I help Mrs. Dawson every morning."

Oh, great, I thought. Just what we need is Flora putting her two cents' worth into our discussion.

When we got to our room Mrs. Dawson was waiting. "Good morning, children," she said. "Flora, I need to have a private talk with Erin and David today. Would you please take these books to the library for me and then wait there until the bell rings?"

She handed Flora a stack of library books. As Flora went past me toward the door, she whispered, "You're in trou-ble."

David closed the door before we sat down.

I took a deep breath and started talking. "While you were gone yesterday," I said, "those of us who stayed here got an idea. The circus plans to sell Lilly, the elephant, to a place where hunters will pay for the opportunity to shoot her and have her head as a trophy. We don't want that to happen. Our class wants to raise the money, buy Lilly, and send her to an elephant sanctuary where she will be cared for and can roam free with other elephants."

"Mrs. Mapes called the sanctuary," David added, "and they'll take Lilly."

"Dr. Martinez and Mrs. Mapes and I are going to meet with Mr. Hinkley from the circus tomorrow morning," I said, "to decide on a price."

"It will be a huge amount," Mrs. Dawson said. "Thousands of dollars. How can a group of sixth graders raise that kind of money?"

"We'll do it," I said, sounding confident even though I was worried about how we would manage. "We want to plan some fund raisers while we're at school and we hope you will let us do that."

Mrs. Dawson was quiet for a moment. "I did not enjoy the circus yesterday," she said. "You ruined it for me."

"I'm sorry," I said.

"When I watched the wild animals I kept thinking of what you had said, and what those other people on the TV news said, about how the animals are forced to do tricks. I wanted to feel excited about the show the way I had when I was a child, but I couldn't."

"We didn't stay at school to hurt you," I said. "We stayed because we wanted to take a stand against the way the Glitter Tent Circus treats its animals."

"I know that," Mrs. Dawson said. "After the circus I went to my nephew's house and told him what had happened. He said the county fair board has had many complaints from people who saw the newscasts and who object to having this circus in Harborview."

I tried not to smile. I was glad other people felt the way I did and were willing to express their beliefs.

"When I accepted the circus tickets," Mrs. Dawson said, "I truly thought it would be an exciting, magical experience for my entire class."

I said nothing.

"It's hard for me to know that the animals who thrilled me as a child were probably mistreated, too," she said, "only back then people were not as aware of cruelty as we are now."

"I want you to remember the happy times with your grandpa," I said. "I never meant to spoil that."

Mrs. Dawson nodded. "It's past," she said, "and so is yesterday's field trip. Tell me more about this elephant sanctuary."

"Would you like to go to the library and look at the sanctuary's web site?" I asked.

"Yes. If my class is going to buy an elephant, I had better learn all the facts."

It was an effort to walk quietly to the library; I felt like skipping.

Flora looked surprised when the three of us entered. David quickly got the elephant sanctuary information on the computer screen and Mrs. Dawson read it until the bell rang.

When we got back to our room, Mrs. Dawson said, "While some of us were at the circus yesterday, those who stayed behind came up with an idea. Erin, will you please tell everyone about it?"

I explained our plan to buy Lilly and send her to the elephant sanctuary.

"The elephant looked all right to me," said Stan, who had gone to the circus. "One of the trapeze performers rode her in the parade. Later Lilly stood on her back legs and waved a flag with her trunk."

I shuddered, thinking of Lilly's cracked, sore nails and her foot rot. "Putting all of her weight on only her two back feet must be painful," I said.

"She's earning her keep," Stan said. "She does the tricks so she'll get fed."

"She shouldn't have to perform for food," I said. "If she had not been captured and removed from the jungle where she belongs, she would feed and take care of herself the way all elephants do in the wild. She does the tricks because she's afraid of what will happen if she doesn't do them."

"She's an animal," Stan said. "You talk as if she were a person."

"She's an intelligent creature, and she should not have to suffer so that we can be entertained."

"I didn't see any suffering," Stan said, "and I was there. You weren't."

"Did you see the television news last night?" I said. "They showed a video of Lilly's trainer beating her."

"Elephants have thick skin," Stan said. "She probably didn't even feel it."

I could tell that nothing I said was going to change Stan's mind so I didn't argue any longer. If he didn't want to help, we would raise the money without him.

Except for Flora, the other kids who had gone to the circus decided to join us.

Flora said nothing. I think she was confused because Mrs. Dawson had been in favor of the circus the day before and now she was cooperating with our plan to rescue Lilly. People like Flora are unable to think for themselves.

Mrs. Dawson said that as soon as we finished our history assignment we could spend our time deciding on ways to raise money. We all—even Pinkie—opened our history books.

By the time school was out that afternoon, everyone but Stan and Flora had pledged to work all weekend and bring their profits on Monday.

"Now all we have to do," David said, "is find out how much Mr. Hinkley wants for Lilly."

Mrs. Mapes offered to pick me up on Saturday. "Wear a dress," she told me. "Look as grown-up as possible."

When she arrived, Dr. Martinez was with her. The

three of us went to the fairgrounds, parked, and found the trailer with a sign that said MANAGER. Mrs. Mapes carried a file folder with some papers in it.

"No matter what he says to us," Dr. Martinez said as we approached the trailer, "be polite. Don't lose your temper."

I could tell that Dr. Martinez did not expect to like Mr. Hinkley any more than I did.

11

The Meanest Man in the World

Mrs. Mapes knocked on the trailer door.

"It isn't locked," said a voice from inside.

Mrs. Mapes pushed open the door; Dr. Martinez and I followed her into the trailer.

Mr. Hinkley sat at a table that held piles of papers, an overflowing ashtray, a plate with dried-up egg stuck to it, and two half-full coffee cups. Penny-size pieces of mold floated in the cold coffee. The room smelled of stale smoke and bacon grease.

Dr. Martinez introduced himself, Mrs. Mapes, and me. I noticed that he simply called himself Bill Martinez rather than using his title.

"Harold Hinkley," the man said. He didn't stand up or offer to shake hands. "Have a seat."

The table was attached to the wall with built-in seating on either side, like a booth in a restaurant.

Mrs. Mapes and Dr. Martinez slid into the seat across from Mr. Hinkley. I didn't want to sit beside Mr. Hinkley, so I sat on a small couch that faced the table.

"I understand you want to buy my elephant," Mr. Hinkley said.

"That's right," Dr. Martinez said. "We saw a newscast where you said she would be sold soon, and we'd like to know your price."

"Lilly's a valuable animal," Mr. Hinkley said. "I'm probably crazy to let her go."

"How much do you want for her?" Dr. Martinez said.

"Fifteen thousand," Mr. Hinkley said.

I stifled a gasp.

"That seems high," Mrs. Mapes said, "for an elephant who is no longer capable of performing well and who has some medical problems."

"Except for a couple of small scratches," Mr. Hinkley said, "Lilly's in perfect health."

I felt like saying, *Liar, liar, pants on fire,* but of course I didn't.

"I've spoken with Dr. Furlan, the veterinarian who examined Lilly earlier this week," Dr. Martinez said. "Lilly has some deep wounds from a bullhook, and three of those wounds are badly infected."

"No big deal," Mr. Hinkley said. "Every circus elephant gets its skin punctured now and then. It's the only way to make them behave."

You, I thought, *have to be the meanest man in the world.*

As if he sensed my thoughts, Mr. Hinkley nodded at me. "What's the kid doing here?" he asked.

"Erin and her classmates are the ones who will be purchasing Lilly," Mrs. Mapes said.

"Oh, no, you don't," Mr. Hinkley said. "I'm not taking an IOU from a bunch of kids."

"It won't be an IOU," I said, trying to sound polite. "We'll give you cash for Lilly."

"You've got fifteen thousand dollars in cash?"

"We have not yet agreed on a price," Dr. Martinez said.

"If that's too much for you," Mr. Hinkley said, "I'll sell her to my other buyer."

"I spoke with a representative of Big Game, Incorporated yesterday," Dr. Martinez said. "I was told they usually pay about ten thousand dollars for an elephant of Lilly's size and condition."

Mr. Hinkley stubbed out his cigarette angrily. Clearly, he had not expected Dr. Martinez to know how much he could get for Lilly from some other buyer. He lit another cigarette, took a puff, then said, "I'll take twelve thousand. Not a penny less."

"Big Game, Incorporated also told us," Mrs. Mapes said, "that they don't need another elephant right now. It seems lions and zebras are currently more popular with their clients."

"They *might* give you ten thousand for Lilly,"

Dr. Martinez said. "We *will* give you eight thousand."

Harold Hinkley frowned at us as he drummed his fingers on the table. "Nine thousand," he said.

"Sorry," said Mrs. Mapes. "Eight thousand is the best we can do."

"When would you want her?" Mr. Hinkley asked.

"It will take us a while to arrange transportation for Lilly," Dr. Martinez said.

It will take us a while to raise that much money, I thought.

"How long will you be in Harborview?" Mrs. Mapes asked.

"Our last show is June tenth."

I did some quick figuring. *That's only twenty-two days,* I thought. *I can't possibly collect enough money in twenty-two days.*

"Where does the circus go from here?" Mrs. Mapes asked.

"We leave the state the next day."

Mrs. Mapes turned to me. "Do you think you can raise the money by June tenth?"

The idea of raising eight thousand dollars in three weeks seemed nearly impossible but I was not about to let Mr. Hinkley know that.

"Of course we can," I said.

Dr. Martinez looked at a small calendar that he had taken from his wallet. "Since the banks are not open on Sundays," he said, "let's complete the sale on Monday morning, June eleventh."

"What are you kids going to do with an elephant?" Mr. Hinkley asked. "They aren't cheap to feed, you know. Lilly weighs two tons and eats a lot of hay every day."

"We're going to send her to an elephant sanctuary in Tennessee," I said.

"Of all the fool ideas I ever heard," Mr. Hinkley said, "that one takes the cake. Have you thought what you could buy for eight thousand dollars?"

Yes, I thought. *I can buy freedom for Lilly.* Out loud I said, "Yes, sir. I want to buy your elephant. It isn't just me; my whole class will earn the money."

Mr. Hinkley's eyes narrowed. His fingers drummed some more. He ground out the cigarette. A fly buzzed over the table, then landed on the sticky plate. I resisted the urge to shoo it off.

"You have a deal," he said, "on one condition. There will be no publicity about this. None. No newspaper stories, no TV news reports, no radio talk shows. Nothing. I have enough problems with animal protection groups as it is. I don't want every television crew in the country hanging around out here doing mushy stories about how a bunch of schoolkids are raising money to send an elephant to a retirement home."

My palms felt sweaty. I had been counting on Jill Gentile to tell about our project on the news, which I knew would result in contributions for

Lilly, and David planned to contact the local newspaper about doing a feature story. Without publicity, my class would have a hard time raising the money.

"Erin?" Mrs. Mapes said. "Do you accept Mr. Hinkley's condition of no publicity?"

"Yes," I said. What else could I say? If I refused, he wouldn't let us buy Lilly.

"I'll need a down payment to hold the elephant for you," Mr. Hinkley said. "Nonrefundable."

"We came prepared for that," Dr. Martinez said. He put five one-hundred-dollar bills on the table.

I gulped. Nonrefundable meant if we didn't have the rest of the money on time, Mr. Hinkley could keep the five hundred dollars.

Mrs. Mapes took the papers from her file folder, then wrote in the blank spaces. "We'll need your signature on this receipt for the money," she said, after she had filled in the amount, "and on this contract for the purchase of Lilly."

"Oh, no." Mr. Hinkley held up both hands as if to keep us away from him. "No receipts and no contracts. Nothing in writing. When I do business, it's a gentleman's agreement, sealed with a handshake. You trust me and I trust you."

Dr. Martinez and Mrs. Mapes glanced at each other as if wondering what to say next. I knew how much they trusted Harold Hinkley: not one bit.

I opened my purse, took out the business card

from David's dad, and handed it to Mr. Hinkley. "Mr. Roderick Showers is the attorney representing our group," I said. "He told us we need to have a contract and signed receipts or the sanctuary won't take Lilly."

"Attorney?" Mr. Hinkley said. He picked up the card and held it by one corner, as if he feared it was covered with germs. "You kids got yourselves a lawyer?"

"Yes, sir," I said.

"That was a senseless thing to do." He dropped the card on the table. "You'll pay more for his fees than you're paying for the elephant."

"Mr. Showers isn't charging us," I said. "He wants us to get Lilly because he's particularly interested in animal cruelty cases."

Mr. Hinkley stared at me.

I stared back, unblinking.

"Where do I sign?" he said.

Mrs. Mapes read the contract out loud, including the eight-thousand-dollar price and the fact that there would be no publicity. Then she showed him where to sign. Mr. Hinkley scrawled his name.

I signed where it said "Sixth Grade Class Representative," then Mrs. Mapes and Dr. Martinez signed, too, since I'm under twenty-one and we wanted the contract to be legally binding.

We each signed three copies. Mr. Hinkley kept one, and Mrs. Mapes took the other two.

No publicity, I thought. How in the world could we raise that much money without publicity?

"Our veterinarian would like to start treating Lilly right away," Mrs. Mapes said. "There'll be no cost to you."

"Sure. Tell him he can doctor any of my animals he wants to, as long as there's no charge."

Mr. Hinkley folded the money and stuffed it in his pants pocket.

As we stood to leave, Dr. Martinez said, "I'd like to see Erin's elephant. Where is she?"

"I don't have time to give tours," Mr. Hinkley said, "but if you want to take a look, she's back by the big silver unit." He pointed toward the rear of the fairgrounds.

I was glad to leave the stale air of the trailer. As we walked toward the back of the fairgrounds, Mrs. Mapes said, "How does it feel to buy an elephant, Erin?"

"It'll feel better," I said, "when she's paid for. Thanks for lending us the down payment, Dr. Martinez."

"It wasn't a loan, it was a contribution: half from me and half from Mrs. Mapes."

"Thank you both," I said.

"Now you only have to raise seventy-five hundred dollars more," Mrs. Mapes said.

"Only," I said, but I felt honored that my teacher and my principal trusted me and my classmates so much that they donated their own money as a non-refundable down payment.

We found Lilly near her travel trailer. Her legs were chained to the iron posts, as they had been the night I first saw her.

Lilly swayed gently from side to side.

"When an elephant rocks back and forth like that," I said, "it means she is frustrated or scared."

"I don't blame her," Dr. Martinez said.

"Hello, Lilly," I said softly. "We're going to rescue you."

I wondered if Mrs. Mapes and Dr. Martinez would think I was silly for talking to an elephant but when I looked at them, Mrs. Mapes had tears in her eyes and Dr. Martinez was smiling at me.

"She can't even turn around or lie down," Mrs. Mapes said, "and that tub of water is filthy."

"I see the cracked nails that Dr. Furlan mentioned," Dr. Martinez said. "He told me her front legs hurt from the infected wounds behind her knees."

I looked at Lilly. I couldn't see the wounds, but the nails on her feet were split and sore looking. No wonder she had not wanted to go down the ramp from her travel trailer to the ground; it probably hurt her to walk.

"As soon as I get home," Mrs. Mapes said, "I'll call Dr. Furlan and ask him to come and start Lilly's treatment."

I took my camera out of my purse and shot some pictures of Lilly, including two close-ups of her feet.

"You'll feel better soon," I told Lilly, "and in twenty-two days, you'll be out of here for good."

I felt Dr. Martinez's hand on my shoulder. "Let's go," he said. "You have work to do."

What an understatement! I needed seven thousand, five hundred dollars, I had to get it in only three weeks, and I couldn't use any publicity.

As we got back into the car, Mrs. Mapes said, "It's up to you now, Erin. Where will you start?"

"Mr. Hinkley said no newspapers, no radio, and no TV," I said, "but he didn't say anything about word-of-mouth advertising. I'm going to call every kid in my class and tell them exactly what the agreement is. Then they can tell other people, and the word will spread that we're raising money to buy Lilly."

"Go, girl," said Mrs. Mapes.

12

Sore Ears and Stiff Muscles

David and Kathleen were waiting on the front steps when I got home.

"What happened?" David asked.

"We can buy Lilly," I said, "if we can raise seventy-five hundred dollars in three weeks."

"Yikes!" said Kathleen.

"The total price is eight thousand. Mrs. Mapes and Dr. Martinez each donated two hundred fifty dollars for the down payment."

"Let's call Jill Gentile right now," David said. "We need help fast."

"We can't," I said. "Mr. Hinkley will sell Lilly to us only if we don't advertise what we are doing. No TV coverage, no newspaper articles, no radio broadcasts. He's afraid if we get a bunch of publicity it will make his circus look bad."

"His circus *is* bad," Kathleen said. "That's why Lilly needs to get out of there."

"If we don't publicize our fund raisers," David said, "nobody will come."

"Our publicity will come from talking to people," I said. "I took some pictures of Lilly. We can show those to everyone we meet and ask for help."

"Was she chained?" David asked.

"Yes. Anyone who sees those pictures will want to help set Lilly free. I dropped off the film on the way home; the pictures will be ready at five o'clock."

"Nana's here," Kathleen said. "She got discharged this morning and she's going to stay with us for a few days."

I ran inside to see my grandma. She and Mom and Dad wanted to hear all about the meeting with Mr. Hinkley.

"You should contact the senior center," Nana suggested. "Many older folks need help with household chores. If they know you're donating the money to a worthy cause, they'll be glad to hire you."

"I'll pay you to weed the garden," Dad said.

Much as I wanted to hop into my jeans and start pulling weeds to earn money for Lilly, I knew I first had to call as many people as I could. I needed to get all of my classmates working at the same time.

I spent so much time that afternoon on the telephone that my ears got sore and sweaty. I had to keep wiping off the receiver with a towel.

By three o'clock I had talked to every kid in my

class I could reach, except Stan, and left messages for several others to call me or David.

Jason said we could do our car wash at his dad's gas station. He offered to schedule workers and be in charge.

When I told Randy about Nana's suggestion, he said he wanted to head that project because his grandpa was active at the senior center.

Chelsea suggested we do snack sales during lunch and recess at school. She said she would call Mrs. Mapes to get permission.

I got a three-ring binder and used a separate page for each money-raising project so that I would have a record of what everyone had agreed to do.

Kathleen offered to organize a fund raiser at the high school. While I was on the phone calling my classmates, she went over to her friend Barb's house.

When she got home she said, "We're having a raffle. We talked to First Class Limousine Service and they agreed to donate a limousine ride on prom night."

"What a fantastic idea," I said. "Every junior and senior in Harborview will want to ride to the prom in a limousine."

Kathleen held up a fistful of bright red tickets. "Barb and I made the raffle tickets on her computer and we'll start selling them at school on Monday. Some other friends are going to sell them, too."

"Thanks," I said. "It's really nice of you to help."

"While you're weeding the garden," Kathleen

replied, "you can help me think of a good slogan for Mama Moo's Strawberry Shakes."

I groaned. "I don't even like Mama Moo's Strawberry Shakes. I think she uses fake strawberries, artificial sweetener, and imitation ice cream. Blah!"

Kathleen waved the raffle tickets at me.

"Oh, all right," I said. "I'll try."

It was hard to think about strawberry shakes, though, because my head was so full of plans for buying Lilly.

As I yanked weeds, Beanie stomped around, trying to get my attention. He's an indoor cat except when I take him out to play, which had not been often lately. I quit weeding and petted him for a few minutes. When I stopped petting, he flopped down on his side and rolled around in the dirt, clearly enjoying himself.

I thought of Lilly, chained in her small trailer.

"I want Lilly to be able to walk in the grass whenever she wants to," I told Beanie. I smiled as I imagined Lilly roaming free on hundreds of acres of woods and pasture. "I want her to wade in a pond, and eat wild bamboo, and wallow in mudholes."

Beanie purred, as if the idea of Lilly's freedom made him happy, too.

Kathleen came out to see if I had thought of a slogan yet.

"You'll never lose with Mama Moo's," I said.

Kathleen wrinkled up her nose.

"It's the best I could do," I said.

"That's okay. I don't really want to win fifty cases of Mama Moo's Strawberry Shakes anyway."

"Yes, you do," I said.

"I thought you didn't like them."

"I don't, but somebody must. We can sell them and use the money for Lilly."

"The contest deadline is tomorrow."

While I had some juice and crackers, I doodled with slogans. Ten minutes later I told Kathleen, "Mind your mama. Drink Moo's strawberry shakes."

Kathleen giggled. "Mind your mama," she said. "That's catchy."

"It's been a long time since you've won anything," I said.

"I'm overdue," Kathleen agreed. "I should win again soon."

I looked at one of the raffle tickets.

RIDE TO THE PROM IN A LIMOUSINE

Be the envy of all your friends
$5 per ticket
All proceeds go to buy Lilly, the circus elephant, and send her to live in an elephant sanctuary

LIMOUSINE DONATED BY FIRST CLASS LIMOUSINE SERVICE

"This raffle was truly inspired thinking," I said.

"Too bad there isn't a contest for raffle ideas," Kathleen said.

I weeded until five, then went to pick up the pictures of Lilly. They turned out great. Her eyes had a hopeless expression, and the chains clearly showed. Even the close-ups of her sore feet were clear. I had ordered double prints, so I mailed one set to the elephant sanctuary, along with the tapes that Andrea had given me of the newscasts.

I took the pictures next door and showed them to David.

"I have two lawn-mowing jobs for tomorrow," he told me. "Ten dollars each."

"I hope everyone else is working as hard as we are," I said. "I already have a sore ear from talking on the phone and stiff muscles from weeding, and this is only the first day."

"Let's make a big chart, like the one Mrs. Dawson had for the book challenge," David said. "That way we can record our progress at school every morning."

We took the chart, the pictures of Lilly, and my three-ring binder to school on Monday. We went early and taped the chart in the hall next to the school office.

Dr. Martinez saw us. "You probably should ask an adult to keep the money for you," he said.

"Will you do it?" I asked.

"Perhaps Mrs. Dawson would do it."

I knew that Dr. Martinez wanted to get Mrs. Dawson involved as a way to smooth her feelings over the sit-in. "I'll ask her," I said.

To my relief, Mrs. Dawson agreed to be our treasurer. I gave her the twenty dollars I had earned by pulling weeds. Lots of other kids brought money, too.

Mrs. Dawson took a fresh tablet from her desk, recorded each name on a separate page, then wrote down the amount that person had brought.

"If it turns out that you don't have enough to buy the elephant," she said, "each of you will get your money back."

All except Dr. Martinez and Mrs. Mapes, I thought. I didn't want to think of that possibility.

As each student turned in the money, he or she told how it was earned. Judy had washed three dogs. Andrea picked strawberries at a berry farm, then sold them to neighbors for a profit. Scooter polished all the silver for his mother's catering service. Several kids had mowed grass or pulled weeds or baby-sat.

Randy said, "My dad said if I would decorate a jar or can that can be used to collect money, he would put it on the counter at the veterinary clinic. I painted a picture of Lilly and glued it on a one-pound coffee can. Then I cut a slit in the plastic lid. Dad took it to the clinic this morning."

"My grandma says she'll make a donation," Andrea said, "but she wants to know who to make the check to."

"I need to speak to someone at the bank," Mrs. Dawson said. "I'll call during our lunch break."

Pinkie amazed us by bringing a book about elephants to school. "I read this yesterday," he said. "Did you know that when an elephant is happy, it makes a purring sound?"

Then he astonished us even more by turning in seventy dollars! "I've been saving to buy a mountain bike," he explained, "but I would not enjoy riding my bike knowing that Lilly was still in chains. I'd rather help her have a reason to purr."

We gave Pinkie a standing ovation. For the second time that school year, Pinkie glowed with pride.

It was thrilling to see how hard everyone had worked. When we added up all the money, it totaled three hundred fifteen dollars. That seemed like a lot until we marked it on the chart.

"We still have a long way to go," said David.

"You'll never make it," said Stan.

"Yes, we will," I said. "We haven't had any of the official fund raisers yet."

The three-ring binder now contained these entries:

Page 1

SIXTH GRADE CAR WASH

Next Saturday at Mr. Jurrey's gas station

Chairperson: Jason Jurrey

Page 2

SENIOR CENTER CHORE PROJECT

Chairperson: Randy Furlan

Willing to work: Erin, David, Andrea, Pinkie, Judy, Greg, Winnie, Michelle, Linda, and Bob

Randy will coordinate jobs with workers.

Page 3

HIGH SCHOOL RAFFLE: limousine ride on prom night

In charge: Kathleen and Barb

Page 4

SCHOOL FOOD SALES

Chairperson: Chelsea Fynch

Faculty advisor: Mrs. Mapes

Mrs. Mapes will purchase granola bars, fruit juice, popcorn, and licorice in bulk quantities at a discount store. We can sell these during lunch hour and afternoon recess.

Mrs. Mapes warned that we would make a slim profit on food sales, but since it was the only money-making activity we could think of that we could do during school hours, we decided to proceed.

"A little profit is better than nothing," I said.

Now that Mrs. Dawson had given her support to the elephant project, even Flora agreed to help.

Mrs. Dawson called the bank, then reported that the bank would open a special account. "Checks can be made to the Lilly Fund," she said. "I'll make a deposit each day after school and we'll earn a small amount of interest until the money is withdrawn."

When Kathleen got home that afternoon, she handed me sixty-five dollars. "I'll have a lot more tomorrow," she promised. "Lots of people wanted to buy a raffle ticket but didn't have enough money with them. Now that everyone knows about the limousine ride, these tickets are a hot item."

Snack sales started the next day and business was brisk. We taped a picture of Lilly to the cash box, and soon the whole school was talking about how Mrs. Dawson's class was trying to rescue an elephant.

During afternoon recess, younger kids asked if they could help. We accepted all offers.

We also heard some crazy rumors. One boy thought we were buying the entire circus. Another believed that after we got Lilly she would be tied in the playground and be the Harborview School mascot.

A fifth grader I barely knew stopped me in the hall and said she had heard about my elephant, and her church youth group wanted to help at our fund raisers. She said if Mr. Jurrey would let us do a second car wash a week after the first one, her group would work.

Each morning Mrs. Dawson collected and recorded the money that we earned for Lilly. Two kids gathered aluminum cans and took them to a recycle center. Michelle sewed doll blankets and sold them at her mother's gift shop. Lots of kids did baby-sitting or pet care or yard work.

Every afternoon we added the profit from that day's snack sales. Gradually, the total increased.

Kathleen's raffle earned the most money in the first few days. Word of the limousine ride spread to the other high school in town and students there wanted tickets.

On Wednesday evening, Kathleen and Barb printed out more tickets.

Every day after we watched Mrs. Dawson total our earnings, we settled right down to do our lessons. Even Pinkie did his schoolwork promptly so that he could join the discussions about our money-raising plans. Working together to buy Lilly made it easy to work on math and spelling.

Before we left school on Friday afternoon we

added in that day's snack sales. We now had six hundred twenty dollars.

Everyone cheered. Judy and Greg went to update our chart, so the rest of the school could see the results.

"Don't forget the car wash tomorrow," Jason said as the bell rang. "Tell all your neighbors to come."

Then, just when it seemed that practically the whole town wanted to help buy Lilly, things started to go wrong.

13

Pickets with Pamphlets

The call came after dinner on Friday.

"It's for you," Kathleen said, handing me the phone. "A man."

"Hello?"

"Is this the kid who wants to buy the elephant?"

"Yes. Who is this?"

"It's Harold Hinkley. The deal's off."

"Off! Why? What happened?"

"I warned you—no publicity."

"We haven't done anything to get publicity."

"No? Then why are there pickets out in front of the circus entrance with signs that say 'Free the Elephant'?"

I sat down, clutching the telephone. Had some well-meaning kids decided to picket the circus? I had stressed to everyone the importance of no publicity, but I knew how easily facts can get twisted or lost when lots of people are repeating the information.

"Are the pickets my age?" I asked.

"They're adults, old enough to know better."

"That isn't my group," I said. "I don't know anything about the pickets."

"They're walking up and down, handing out pamphlets and intimidating my customers."

"It isn't my classmates," I said. "You can't back out of our agreement because of what someone else does. I have no control over those people."

"If it isn't your group, then who is it?" he asked.

"I don't know. Why don't you ask them?"

"I'm not going out there. Some fool would likely take a shot at me."

"A shot!" I said. "Are the pickets carrying guns?"

"I didn't see any guns," Mr. Hinkley admitted, "but you never know with those animal fanatics."

"People who care about animals," I said, trying to calm him down, "are usually gentle and loving. Most would never use violence."

"I want them out of here," he said.

"Have you called the police?" I asked.

"I don't like cops."

"I'm afraid I can't help you," I said. "Those pickets have nothing to do with me or my school or our contract to buy Lilly."

Clunk! He hung up on me without saying goodbye.

I hurried over to David's house and told him about the call.

"Let's go over there ourselves and see who's picketing," he said.

We rode our bikes to the fairgrounds where a dozen people were walking up and down with signs. Only two of the signs said FREE THE ELEPHANT. The others said YOU HAVE A CHOICE—THE ANIMALS DON'T! or TEACH KINDNESS, NOT CRUELTY or JUNGLE ANIMALS BELONG IN THE JUNGLE.

One of the pickets saw us and held out a pamphlet.

It was a list of ways to tell if a circus animal had been mistreated, and a request to watch for evidence of abuse when attending the circus. People were asked to report any signs of mistreatment to STAC.

"If Mr. Hinkley had bothered to come out and read one of these pamphlets," I said, "he would have known what organization the pickets represent."

"I don't see Nancy or Mike," David said as he looked at the other pickets.

"Why are you carrying 'Free the Elephant' signs?" I asked the woman who had given me the pamphlet.

"One of our group took video of the trainer beating the elephant," she said.

"We saw that on the television news," David said.

"We want the circus to give Lilly to a good zoo or an animal sanctuary," the woman said.

"I have a favor to ask of you," I said.

She looked surprised.

Quickly I explained that we were trying to buy Lilly and send her to a sanctuary. I told her how much money we needed, and that we couldn't have any publicity.

"Mr. Hinkley, the circus manager, called me a little while ago," I said. "He saw your signs about the elephant and accused me of breaking my promise not to publicize what we're doing. I told him my group had nothing to do with the picketing but he didn't believe me."

"You want us to leave?" she asked. I could tell by the way she asked that she had no intention of going.

"No," I said. "I just want you to put away the 'Free the Elephant' signs. They're making a problem for us that might end up hurting Lilly."

"I don't want that awful man to think we'll do what he says," the woman said.

"He isn't asking this, I am. For Lilly."

She nodded. "All right," she said. She explained our request to the other people who were picketing. "We can't expect the circus to give away the elephant," she told them, "no matter how much pressure we apply. But they might sell her to these children, so we need to back off and give the kids a chance."

Everyone agreed.

"Thanks," I said, "and thanks for being here to try to help the animals."

"Good luck," she replied. "If STAC had any money, we'd give you some."

As soon as we got home, I called Mr. Hinkley. "This is Erin Wrenn," I said. "I went to the fairgrounds and spoke with the pickets."

"You said you didn't know them."

"I don't. They're from a group called STAC. I told them our contract says no publicity and they agreed not to carry the elephant signs anymore."

"They're still out there, marching up and down and handing out leaflets. They still have signs."

"I can't make them stop picketing, but I did ask them not to carry the signs about Lilly."

"I'll let you get away with it this time," Mr. Hinkley said, "but if there's any more publicity, you've lost your down payment, and the elephant."

He hung up before I could respond.

When the dial tone buzzed in my ear, I slammed the receiver down.

"What a jerk!" I said. I mimicked him for David: "I'll let you get away with it this time."

I flopped down on the couch. "I think he's looking for a reason to get out of the contract and keep the down payment. He made such a point of saying it was nonrefundable."

"He could keep our five hundred dollars," David said, "then sell Lilly to someone else."

"We have to raise that money as fast as we can," I said, "before Mr. Hinkley weasels out of the deal."

"I don't see how we can work any faster," David said. He changed to his announcer's voice. "A student collapsed of exhaustion Friday night," he said, "after pulling weeds every day after school. He was revived in the nick of time by a friend who offered him a root beer float." He gave me a hopeful look.

As I poured root beer into our glasses, I said, "I'm glad tomorrow's Saturday. Between the car wash, the senior center work day, and all the individual jobs that people have lined up, we should make a bundle."

We didn't, though.

It rained on Saturday.

14

Not Enough Money

When I woke up and heard raindrops hitting the roof, I felt like crying.

Nobody would come to a car wash in the rain. David couldn't mow lawns in a downpour. Much of the work that the senior center had arranged was outdoors, too, including one job painting a garage, for which we would be paid one hundred dollars. What about all the yard work that other kids had promised to do?

Glumly I turned on my radio to get a weather report. "Mostly rain today," the announcer said, "with a chance of partial clearing by evening."

We held the car wash anyway, and a few people came. I think they felt sorry for us.

The grass didn't get cut, but a few kids pulled weeds in the rain. Some of the senior citizens who had signed up for yard work gave the workers indoor jobs instead. The garage painting got postponed for a week, and Mr. Jurrey said we could schedule another car wash for the next Saturday.

After dinner, David and I went to the fairgrounds to see how many people were going to the circus. The crowd seemed sparse, and I wondered if the newscast about cruelty charges had made a difference. The STAC group was there, minus the elephant signs, handing out their checklists.

We couldn't get past the gate without buying a ticket, but we rode our bikes to the back of the fairgrounds, and looked through the fence at Lilly's trailer. We didn't see Lilly.

On Sunday Nana paid me to wash all her windows on the inside, and Aunt Lorna hired me to watch Misty for a couple of hours. Then I baked two batches of chocolate-chip cookies to take to school for Monday's snack sale.

The cookies had been Andrea's idea. "We'd make more profit if we could get free food," she said. She suggested that we ask grocery stores for donations or bring home-baked cookies.

The money we turned in on Monday was far less than we had hoped it would be. Although all the kids had done their best, the rain had spoiled a lot of plans. The only big amount came from Kathleen's raffle tickets: four hundred sixty dollars.

When we added the weekend numbers to what we

already had, our total was twelve hundred eighty dollars.

"If you do that well on a rainy weekend," Mrs. Dawson said, "think how much you will earn next Saturday and Sunday."

I knew she was trying to be upbeat so we wouldn't get discouraged.

Will we be able to earn enough money? I wondered. *What if it rained again?* For the first time since I had signed the contract with Mr. Hinkley, I began to have serious doubts about whether I could fulfill my part of the bargain.

My classmates and I worked every waking moment that week. We did chores for the seniors, for neighbors, and for relatives. We sold snacks at school. Randy brought forty dollars from his collection can.

I baked cookies every night after dinner. I told Mom and Dad they didn't need to give me any allowance that month, to make up for all the ingredients I used.

Dad gave it to me anyway. "You can donate it to the cause," he said, and he gave me ten dollars extra.

The second Saturday was a glorious, sunny day. Cars lined up to get into Mr. Jurrey's gas station for our car wash. We stayed an extra two hours in order to wash every car that came. We asked for a five-dollar donation but many people gave us tips.

Six kids got the senior center client's garage painted before noon, and then did chores for other seniors. David mowed four lawns in one day. I got up at six in order to bake two batches of peanut butter cookies, which I sold for fifty cents each to people who were waiting at the car wash.

By Monday the Lilly Fund totaled three thousand one hundred forty-five dollars. It was less than half the amount we needed, and we had only one week left.

On Tuesday David brought four hundred dollars to school. "I offered my lawn-mowing clients a special deal," he said. "I charge ten dollars to mow the lawn. I told them that if they would pay me for ten times in advance, they'd get the eleventh time free. Four people agreed, and I had them make their checks to the Lilly Fund."

"Way to go!" Pinkie shouted.

"I'll be cutting grass the rest of the summer with no further pay," David said, "but we need the money now."

Two other kids who did yard work decided to ask their customers to pay in advance.

My hopes went up again.

From then on, my emotions were like a roller-coaster ride. When someone turned in an unexpectedly large amount, my spirits soared; when the amounts were only five or ten dollars and the red line on the chart barely moved, I despaired.

I baked more cookies Wednesday night. Thursday would be the final day of snack sales because Friday was the last day of school, and we got out at noon.

"I hope you won't be too disappointed if you can't raise enough money to buy Lilly," Mom said, as she watched me put the cookies on a rack to cool. "That's a huge sum to earn in a very short time."

"We have to do it," I said. "If we don't, Mr. Hinkley will keep our down payment and Lilly will be sold to that awful place where hunters come in and shoot the animals." I struggled to keep back tears.

"You're tired," Mom said. "You should go to bed."

I hate it when she says that, especially because she is usually right.

I *was* tired—tired of working every minute, tired of worrying about Lilly, and tired of being in charge of the whole project. When there were problems such as the rain that first Saturday, the other kids called me to ask what they were supposed to do. They called and wanted to know how much to charge for certain chores. Someone even called to ask if donations were tax deductible.

"No," I said. "We are not a nonprofit corporation; we're just a group of kids."

Although I had tried to delegate responsibility by having other people head the different fund raisers, ultimately I was the one they turned to with questions or when anything went wrong. Buying Lilly had been my idea, and no matter how weary I was, I was still the leader.

On Thursday, after we added the final lunch hour snack sales, our total stood at four thousand, two hundred forty dollars.

"We need a miracle," Andrea said.

"We need a loan," I replied.

"Who would lend money to a bunch of kids?"

"Maybe the bank will," I said. "That's what banks do, isn't it? We can borrow the amount we need, then we'll continue to have fund raisers during the summer until we pay it off."

After some discussion, it was agreed that Jason, Andrea, Pinkie, David, and I would go to the bank that had the Lilly Fund account and apply for an elephant loan.

"We need three thousand, two hundred sixty dollars more," I said, "but we'll earn some money this weekend, even if it rains again. Let's ask to borrow three thousand dollars."

"Since school gets out at noon tomorrow," Mrs. Dawson said, "you may go to the bank in the morning so that you can report back to the class while everyone is still here."

We met at the bank at ten o'clock. I hardly recognized Pinkie in a white shirt and necktie. David's dad had helped him write a proposal the night before so that we had something official looking to present. I took along the contract to buy Lilly.

As we passed the automatic teller machine outside the bank's front door, Jason said, "When I was little, I thought the ATMs gave out free money. I'd see my mom put in her little card and get back twenty-dollar bills. I could hardly wait until I was old enough to have a card and get my free money."

"If only it were that simple," I said.

The banker, Mr. Kox, greeted us cordially, shook hands with each of us, and took us into a small room where we could all sit around a table. "Now then," he said when we were all seated, "what can I do for you?"

"We need to borrow three thousand dollars," I said. I explained about Lilly, and showed him our agreement with Mr. Hinkley.

Andrea and Jason told about the fund raisers. Pinkie said he planned to continue to earn money all summer. David handed Mr. Kox a copy of our formal proposal for the loan.

Mr. Kox studied it for a moment. Then he said, "I wish I could help you, but I can't. You are a fine group of young people but you are not what my bank would consider a good credit risk."

I looked down at my lap.

"When I approve a loan," Mr. Kox said, "I'm not lending my own money; I'm lending the money of customers who have deposited it with me. They count on me to earn as much interest as possible and to make only sound investments that have no chance of failure."

"We'll pay back the loan," David said. "Our whole class has agreed to work this summer."

"Good intentions can fail," Mr. Kox said. "When school is out for the summer your group won't see each other regularly to coordinate your efforts. If the elephant is freed before she's paid for, it may be much more difficult to motivate people to earn the money."

He's right, I thought. It would be lots harder to stay organized during summer vacation.

"If I approved this loan and you didn't pay it back," Mr. Kox said, "the loss would come from my other customers' profits. I'm sorry; I can't take that chance."

I stood. "Thanks for talking to us," I said.

David picked up the proposal.

"Perhaps one of you could ask your parents to lend you the money," Mr. Kox suggested.

We walked through the bank lobby and out the door.

As we headed toward the school, we discussed Mr. Kox's idea.

"My folks don't have that kind of money to lend," Pinkie said. "We can barely pay the rent every month."

"I want this to be our own project," Randy said,

"something we pull off without having our parents bail us out."

"He had a point about keeping everyone motivated during vacation," David said. "What if we borrowed the money and then we're the only ones who keep working to pay off the loan?"

"We could spend all summer doing nothing but work," Andrea said, "and still not have enough."

Dr. Martinez was waiting in our classroom to find out what had happened at the bank.

"We talked to Mr. Kox, the bank's manager," I said. "He won't lend us the money."

Disappointment settled over the class like thick fog.

"I guess we've lost, then," Linda said.

"Not yet," I said. "We still have tonight and tomorrow and Sunday. We can ask some new people to help. We can earn a lot of money in three days."

"I can't work after today," Greg said. "My family leaves on vacation tomorrow morning."

"I'll be gone, too," Scooter said. "I'm flying to my grandparents' house this afternoon."

"There are still plenty of kids available," Jason said. "The church group will be at the car wash again tomorrow."

"What's our absolute deadline, Erin?" Chelsea asked.

"The truck from the elephant sanctuary is due to arrive Monday afternoon to get Lilly," I said. "I'm meeting with Mr. Hinkley that morning to pay him the rest of the money."

"Let's meet here at school Sunday night," Judy said, "to total our earnings from the weekend. If we don't have enough, we can decide then what to do next."

"I can come at seven," Mrs. Dawson said, "to let you in."

"Get everyone you know to work for Lilly between now and Sunday night," I said. "We can still do it!"

I knew I was probably being unrealistic, but I couldn't give up when we had come so far.

My optimism was contagious. Usually on the last day of school, everyone rushes away yelling, "Goodbye! See you in September." This year, kids clustered in groups, planning additional ways to earn money for Lilly.

"Get your brothers and sisters and cousins involved," I said. "Get everyone you know to help."

As soon as I got home, I asked Kathleen if she would donate baby-sitting money or whatever else she could earn for this final weekend of fund raising.

"Gee, I'm sorry," Kathleen said. "Barb's family invited me to go camping with them this weekend. They're picking me up in an hour and I won't be back until Sunday night."

I swallowed my disappointment. Kathleen had

already raised hundreds of dollars with her raffle; it wouldn't be fair to ask her to stay home from a fun camping trip.

Friday night I baked cookies to sell at the car wash. I no longer needed a recipe; by then I could have baked cookies blindfolded.

"I'll be sorry when this project ends," Dad said as he helped himself to an oatmeal cookie. "Our house smells like a bakery."

The Saturday car wash earned four hundred dollars, including thirty dollars from my cookies. Mr. Jurrey came out as we wound up the hoses and put our pails and rags away. "If you want to have another car wash tomorrow afternoon," he said, "you're welcome to do it."

"I'll come back tomorrow," Chelsea said.

"I can come," Pinkie said.

I was scheduled to do yard work for Aunt Lorna but I was pretty sure I could go there early and finish in time to help at the car wash. We agreed to wash cars again, starting at one.

By five o'clock Sunday afternoon, as I coiled the hoses for the last time, I was so tired I could have fallen asleep right there next to Mr. Jurrey's gasoline pumps. I didn't think there could be a dirty car left in the entire town.

David's dad gave me a ride home. I changed out of my soaking wet clothes, put on dry ones, and ate a peanut butter sandwich.

"You are exhausted," Mom said. "Instead of getting dry clothes, you should put on your pajamas."

"I have to go over to the school at seven," I said. "Mrs. Dawson is meeting us there and we're going to add up everything we earned this weekend."

Mom sighed. "I hope it's enough," she said. "I never saw a group of people work so hard."

Most of my classmates looked as worn out as I felt. Mrs. Dawson unlocked the front door, then opened her classroom. We all trudged in, clutching our profits.

The two car washes had made nearly seven hundred dollars.

Andrea had another check from her grandmother for five hundred dollars. "I have to walk her dog every day for the rest of my life," Andrea said.

Senior chores had netted us three hundred sixty dollars. Individual kids who had done baby-sitting, pet care, yard work, and a variety of other chores turned in four hundred twenty-five dollars.

Mrs. Dawson added everything up, then added the total to our previous earnings. "The grand total," she said, "is six thousand two hundred thirty dollars."

No one spoke. I heard the wall clock ticking away the seconds, and behind me I heard Chelsea sniffle, as she tried not to cry.

The numbers hung in the air as if they were helium balloons.

Six thousand, two hundred thirty dollars.

It was an astonishing amount for a group of sixth graders to raise in only three weeks—but it was not enough to buy Lilly.

We were one thousand two hundred seventy dollars short, and we were out of time.

15

Kathleen's Amazing Letter

Andrea broke the silence. "What are we going to do?"

"I'm going to go home and sleep for a week," Pinkie said. "I've never been so tired."

The others all looked at me, as if I could come up with a magical solution.

"When I see Mr. Hinkley tomorrow," I said, "I'll ask him for an extension of time."

It was the only plan I could think of, but I knew it wouldn't work. Mr. Hinkley would keep the five-hundred-dollar down payment, and he would keep Lilly.

Thanks to Dr. Furlan, Lilly was healthier than she had been when we signed the contract. Mr. Hinkley could probably sell her now for more than what we were going to pay. Why should he give us extra time?

"You had better call the elephant sanctuary and postpone the truck," Pinkie said.

"It's too late," I replied. "The truck is already on its way."

I felt responsible for the sad looks on the faces of my friends. They had worked so hard. They had put their faith in me when I said we could do this, and all their work had been for nothing.

I let everyone down, I thought, including the people at the elephant sanctuary. They believed me when I said my class would buy Lilly. I had told them wishful thinking, and they had accepted it as truth. Now I was wasting sanctuary money by having a truck come to Harborview only to return without an elephant.

Mrs. Dawson slipped into her kindergarten voice. "Tomorrow is a new day," she said, "and things will look better in the morning. Everyone who can, meet back here at noon to find out how much more time we have to raise the money."

Some of the other kids perked up, believing that there was still a chance for us to save Lilly.

I knew better. So did David. We walked slowly home, heads down, without talking. I felt as if someone I loved had just died.

When I went inside, Mom took one look at my face and said, "I'm so sorry, Erin."

"I failed," I said.

"People who attempt something difficult are never failures," Mom said. "The only failures are those who won't try. You gave it your best, and you should be proud of yourself."

"Pride doesn't help Lilly," I said. Then the tears I'd been holding back burst forth like water overflowing a dam. I ran into my room, lay facedown on my bed, and sobbed.

In my mind's eye I saw Lilly's sad eyes and chained feet. I saw her rocking back and forth, back and forth. I imagined the wounds that were healing getting infected again as her trainer continued to use the bullhook. I saw her going from town to town in that cramped, filthy trailer while Mr. Hinkley ignored her suffering. Worst of all, I saw her being shot by a trophy hunter.

I cried until my eyes were red, my nose was sore, and I had the hiccups. Finally I went into the bathroom and splashed cold water on my face.

That's where I was when Kathleen got home from her camping trip. I heard Mom and Dad tell her that I didn't have enough money to buy Lilly.

Next I heard the most incredible shriek.

I dropped the towel and opened the bathroom door as Kathleen shrieked again.

"What is it?" Mom asked.

"I won!" Kathleen shouted. "I won! I won! I won!"

I went into the living room.

Kathleen was jumping up and down, clutching a piece of paper in each hand. One was a letter; the other looked like a check.

"She opened the letter that came for her on Saturday," Mom said.

"Which contest?" I asked. "What did you win?"

"Look!" Kathleen said. She waved the papers at me.

I tried to read them but couldn't because Kathleen was still acting like a Yo-Yo.

"I won second prize for the essay on What I Would Do if I Were President!"

"What did you win?" I repeated. "What's your prize?" I remembered that the first prize in that contest was money, but Kathleen had never said what the other prizes were.

Kathleen beamed at us. "I won . . ." She paused dramatically, dragging out the tension. Then she shouted, "I won four thousand dollars!"

"Four thousand dollars!" Mom said.

"That beats an electric toothbrush," Dad said.

Twenty percent of four thousand, I thought, is eight hundred. It was a huge amount but it was still not enough to save Lilly.

I swallowed and forced myself to smile at my sister. "Congratulations," I said.

Kathleen said, "The judges said they liked how I included less well-known issues, such as the exploitation of exotic animals."

My smile became genuine.

"I've changed my mind about our deal, Erin. Without the part you wrote, I might not have won, so instead of you getting twenty percent, we'll split the prize, fifty-fifty."

My heart throbbed in my throat as I did the math.

Half the prize was two thousand dollars! Half the prize would be enough!

"Are you sure?" I said. The tears started again, only this time they were tears of joy.

"I'm sure," Kathleen said. "You've helped me with practically every contest I've entered. Besides, I'd hate to think I sold all those raffle tickets for nothing. I want Lilly to be free."

I hugged my sister.

I hugged Mom and Dad.

I hugged Beanie.

Then I ran next door and hugged David.

"Hey!" he said, pushing me away. "What did I do?"

"We're buying Lilly!" I said. "We have enough money!"

Somehow I calmed down enough to tell him what had happened.

"We interrupt this program," David said, "with good news. The heartbreaking story of the group who came up short in their efforts to raise money to buy a circus elephant has a happy ending, after all. Due to the literary skill and generosity of two sisters, the elephant will go free!"

"Tomorrow," I said, "Lilly will be ours. Nothing can go wrong now."

I was mistaken about that, but I didn't find it out until the next morning.

16

Unwanted Publicity

I was supposed to meet Mr. Hinkley at ten-thirty Monday morning. I called Mrs. Dawson and Mrs. Mapes Sunday night, to tell them about the prize money. We arranged to meet at the bank at ten-fifteen.

Mom went to the bank with Kathleen and me at ten. Kathleen endorsed her prize check, then put half in a certificate of deposit for her college education.

We put one thousand two hundred seventy dollars in the Lilly Fund, and the rest went into a savings account for my future college costs.

I couldn't stop smiling as I looked at the paperwork. For weeks I had worried about not having enough money to buy Lilly and now I not only had enough to buy the elephant, I had a brand-new savings account.

Mrs. Dawson arrived. Using the money from our weekend's work, plus what was in the Lilly Fund, she got a money order, payable to Mr. Hinkley, for six thousand dollars. The teller put it into a white envelope. Mrs. Dawson also took fifteen hundred in cash, which the teller put into a second white envelope.

My hands trembled when Mrs. Dawson handed the two envelopes to me. "Well done, Erin," she said.

"Thank you for helping us," I replied. "We couldn't have done it without using class time to plan our fund raisers."

"It was a good learning experience," Mrs. Dawson said, "for all of us."

"I hope you do the Three Hundred Books Challenge with your class next year," I said. "It was really fun."

"I've decided to go back to teaching kindergarten," Mrs. Dawson said. "It suits me better."

Mr. Kox came out of his office. Pointing at the bank envelopes in my hand, he said, "I see you were able to borrow the money from your parents."

"No," I said. "We raised it ourselves."

"You kids earned three thousand dollars since you were here?"

"Three thousand two hundred sixty dollars," I said.

Mrs. Mapes and Dr. Martinez drove up in front of the bank. Enjoying Mr. Kox's look of astonishment, I climbed in the back seat.

I gave the two envelopes to Dr. Martinez.

"Why did you want part in cash?" I asked.

"Mr. Hinkley will get the cash after Lilly is picked up by the sanctuary's truck," Mrs. Mapes said. "We didn't think it was wise to give him the full amount before then."

"Not that we don't trust Mr. Hinkley," Dr. Martinez said.

"Of course not," Mrs. Mapes said.

"Ha!" I said.

Dr. Martinez handed a newspaper to me. "Have you seen this?" he asked.

The paper was folded so the second page was on top. The headline jumped out at me: SCHOOL CHILDREN RAISE MONEY TO RESCUE ELEPHANT.

"Oh, no," I said. "Not publicity on the last day!"

Quickly I read the article. It told about the car washes and the raffle. It said we were trying to buy Lilly and send her to a sanctuary. It mentioned STAC's taped evidence of cruelty. Then it quoted two Harborview Elementary School students, one in second grade and one in fourth grade. I didn't know either of them.

"How could this have happened?" I said. "We told everyone that we couldn't have newspaper articles or any other publicity."

Mrs. Mapes said, "I don't remember seeing those girls who were interviewed at any of your fund raisers."

"They didn't help. I don't even know who they are."

"They're nice girls," Dr. Martinez said. "I'm sure they had no idea that we weren't supposed to have a newspaper article."

"What are we going to do?" I asked.

"We're going to hope that Mr. Hinkley doesn't read the morning paper."

Circus workers were dismantling the big tent as we drove in. We parked near Mr. Hinkley's trailer.

"The driver who will be taking Lilly to the sanctuary called last night," Mrs. Mapes said. "He expects to arrive here around two o'clock this afternoon."

The three of us trooped through the dry sawdust to the manager's trailer. I knocked.

"It's open," Mr. Hinkley called.

As soon as I stepped inside, I saw the newspaper article lying on the table in front of him.

"We're here to pay you the rest of the money," I said.

"The deal's off," Mr. Hinkley said. "You promised no publicity."

"This article quotes two kids I never heard of," I said. "They aren't in my class, and they haven't worked on the fund raisers."

"The reporter got accurate information somewhere," Mr. Hinkley said.

"Let's call the newspaper and ask the reporter what happened," Mrs. Mapes said.

"It won't change anything," Mr. Hinkley said. "The damage is done."

"Still, I'm curious as to how this could have happened," Mrs. Mapes said. "Erin and her classmates were so careful not to publicize what they were doing."

She took her cell phone out of her purse. I wondered if she was stalling for time, trying to think of a way to convince Mr. Hinkley to complete the sale.

We all listened as she called the newspaper and asked to speak to the woman whose by-line was on the article.

After the conversation, Mrs. Mapes explained, "The reporter's teenage nephew purchased a raffle ticket for the limousine ride. She saw the ticket, asked about it, and her nephew said some elementary school kids were trying to buy the elephant. Next she called a friend who has two children in Harborview Elementary School."

"The girls who are quoted in the article?" I asked.

"That's right. They confirmed that Mrs. Dawson's class was raising money to save the elephant. Their mother had attended your car wash. The reporter tried to reach Dr. Martinez, but he was not at home and of course school was closed. She felt her sources were reliable, and wrote the story."

"Mr. Hinkley," I pleaded, "you can see that I had nothing to do with this. No one in my group knew about the article."

"This is exactly the sort of story I was worried about," Mr. Hinkley said. "It's why I said 'no publicity' right from the start. I kept my part of the bargain. I let your veterinarian come every day to work on Lilly. I didn't sell her to anyone else."

"I kept the bargain, too," I said. "I never met the girls who talked to the newspaper reporter. There's no way I could have prevented this."

Mr. Hinkley shrugged as if the whole matter was out of his control. "Sorry, kid," he said. "A deal's a deal." He stood up, clearly signifying that our meeting was over.

"You can't cancel our agreement now," I said, trying not to cry. "Not when I kept my word."

"Oh, can't I?" he said. "How are you going to stop me?"

My mind raced as I looked at him. How could I convince him to let me buy Lilly?

"Mr. Hinkley," I said, "if you think this little newspaper article is bad publicity, wait until you see what happens if you refuse to sell Lilly to me."

He narrowed his eyes suspiciously. "What will happen?"

"If you don't take our money, and sign the release, and let the elephant sanctuary truck take Lilly this afternoon, there is going to be more publicity than you have ever seen."

I stood, to put myself more at his eye level. "I'll call this reporter back, and I'll call Jill Gentile at the television station, and the STAC people who were picketing. I'll call the Humane Society."

He stared at me.

"This is exactly the kind of story that gets picked up by the national networks or the Associated Press," Mrs. Mapes said.

"Erin and her friends will be on every radio talk show in the state," Dr. Martinez said.

"If you don't let me buy Lilly," I said, "you'll be lucky to ever sell another ticket to your circus, anywhere."

Dr. Martinez took the money order for six thousand dollars out of the envelope and laid it on the table. He took fifteen one-hundred-dollar bills from the second envelope, and fanned them out in his hand.

"The six thousand is yours now," he said, pushing the money order toward Mr. Hinkley, "and you get the cash this afternoon when Lilly leaves."

I took a deep breath, trying to think clearly, then instantly regretted it. The stale cigarette smell was giving me a headache.

"I don't think a smart businessman like you is going to walk away from this much money," I said, "when the result would be nothing but bad publicity."

Mr. Hinkley stood there glaring at me for a few seconds. I stared right back, refusing to look away. I could hear the shouts of the workers outside as they took down the tents. It seemed impossible that it was less than a month since David and I had watched them go up, the night I first saw Lilly.

At last Mr. Hinkley spoke. "I'm probably crazy to do this," he said. He reached for the money order, read it carefully, then put it into his shirt pocket. "I'm practically giving that valuable elephant away."

"Sign here, please," Mrs. Mapes said. She held a piece of paper and a pen toward Mr. Hinkley.

"Now what?"

"It's a receipt for the six thousand dollars."

"Our attorney requires a receipt," I added.

Mr. Hinkley signed his name where Mrs. Mapes pointed.

"The sanctuary truck will be here at two," I said.

Mr. Hinkley nodded. "You drive a hard bargain, kid," he said.

17

Trunks, Treats, and Tears

That afternoon a custom-built elephant transport trailer, pulled by a truck, arrived at the fairgrounds. Lilly would ride to her new home in style.

Twenty of my classmates came to watch Lilly leave the circus forever. David had called Pinkie, Jason, and Randy the night before, to tell them about the contest prize, and I had called many of the girls. The news had spread like chicken pox.

Mrs. Mapes, Dr. Martinez, and Dr. Furlan came, too. We gave Mr. Hinkley the envelope of cash and watched him sign where it said "Paid in Full."

"Lilly will be comfortable all the way to Tennessee," the driver told us, just before he led her into the trailer. As she walked up the ramp, I thanked Dr. Furlan for helping her to heal.

Lilly examined her new temporary quarters with interest, and did not seem afraid.

"Have you driven other elephants to the sanctuary?" I asked the driver, who was a volunteer professional truck driver who donated his time to help the elephants.

"This is my second. The first time, I stopped often to offer water and carrots, and I'll do the same with Lilly."

As the special trailer drove through the fairgrounds gate, all of us waved and called, "Good-bye, Lilly! Good-bye! Have a happy life!"

I remembered the early trouble with Mrs. Dawson, the sit-in on the day of the field trip, the negotiations with Mr. Hinkley, the weeks of hard work, and the many times I had felt overwhelmed by the responsibility of being in charge.

It was worth it, I thought. All the worry and sore muscles and fear that we wouldn't make our goal were worth it for this one moment of watching Lilly leave, knowing she'll live the rest of her life in peace and freedom.

I thought about how I had almost pretended to be sick on circus day, because it would have been easier than standing up for my beliefs, and how embarrassed I was when the other kids stared at me as I first objected to the circus.

I remembered wishing I didn't have such strong convictions, wishing I were more like Flora.

As I watched Lilly's truck head toward the highway, I didn't wish that anymore.

It's always risky to be the one who stands out, I thought, but if I had not refused to attend the circus, my classmates wouldn't have known about circus animal abuse, and Lilly would still be captive.

Mrs. Mapes put a hand on my shoulder. "You were brilliant this morning, Erin," she said. "Warning Mr. Hinkley about bad publicity was probably the only strategy that would have worked."

"A local girl's brain is being studied by Harvard scientists," David said. "Tune in at six to find out how she got so smart."

I watched until the truck and trailer were out of sight.

When I got home, Kathleen met me at the door.

"I thought you were going to watch Lilly leave," I said.

"I had to stay here to receive a delivery."

"A delivery of what?"

"We won another contest. Come and look."

I followed her into the house, then stopped and stared. Our living room was piled with huge cardboard boxes. Boxes sat on the couch, on the chairs, and on top of the piano.

Each box had bright pink lettering on the side: PETAL PINK TOILET TISSUE—NEW PEPPERMINT SCENT.

"How much is there?" I asked.

"One hundred cartons. Eighty packages of four in each carton."

Kathleen pried open the closest box and tossed me

some pink toilet tissue. "Same deal as before," she said. "It's half yours."

I sniffed the peppermint. "We're on a roll," I said.

Kathleen groaned.

We gave toilet tissue to the shelter for homeless people, to all our friends and neighbors, and to the Boys and Girls Club. There was still so much left we had to store it in the garage and leave our car outside. Thirty-two thousand rolls is a lot of toilet tissue.

Every Saturday for the rest of the summer, I helped David with his prepaid lawn jobs. Since I had received a huge sum of money for half a day's work writing part of an essay, it didn't seem fair for him to mow and weed by himself every Saturday.

Three weeks after we watched Lilly leave, I got a letter from the elephant sanctuary. When I opened it, photos of Lilly fell into my lap.

I looked at a picture of her standing beside a pond, and another of her lying in the grass, taking a nap in the sun.

One picture showed her in a spacious, clean barn, playing with her new toy—a tire. In my favorite picture, Lilly stood with another elephant, their trunks intertwined.

The pictures blurred as happy tears filled my eyes. I brushed them away and began to read.

"Dear Erin," the letter began, "Lilly has adjusted well. She was nervous at first but now she lets the other elephants touch her with their trunks and she grazes with them outside. She flaps her ears when she sees her favorite friend—a sign of contentment.

"She trumpets with the others," the letter continued, "and she's gaining weight. Her cracked nails are growing out and the infected wounds from the bullhook are completely gone. Walking on sand, mud, and grass helps her feet to heal.

"Her favorite treats are carrots and oranges. When we bring those, Lilly turns and presents her back leg to us in greeting."

I read the letter twice, then sat for a long time looking at the pictures. Beanie hopped onto my lap, curled up, and closed his eyes. I stroked his fur.

"Not many people get a chance to save an elephant," I told him, "but I did. I helped save Lilly."

Beanie purred.

I thought of Lilly roaming free with her elephant friends, and I felt like purring myself.

Author's Note

All of the characters in this book, including Lilly the elephant, are fictitious. The Glitter Tent Circus is fictitious, too. However, the information about the unhappy lives of most circus animals is true.

There really are sanctuaries for unwanted elephants. Riddle's Elephant Breeding Farm and Wildlife Sanctuary is a three hundred thirty–acre nonprofit Arkansas wildlife preserve that accepts both Asian and African elephants. Learn more about this sanctuary at www.elephantsanctuary.org or write to P.O. Box 715, Greenbrier, AR 72058.

The Elephant Sanctuary, P.O. Box 393, Hohenwald, TN 38462, is a natural-habitat refuge for endangered Asian elephants. It, too, is a non-profit sanctuary. You can learn more at www.elephants.com.

Thanks to Susan Michaels of Pasado's Safe Haven, an animal rescue and rehabilitation organization (www.pasadosafehaven.com), for helping me write accurately about animal-cruelty laws. Pasado's Safe Haven has waged numerous prosecutions against animal abusers and has won major convictions.

About the Author

PEG KEHRET's books for young readers are regularly recommended by the American Library Association, the International Reading Association, and the Children's Book Council. She has won twenty-one state children's book awards and has also won the Golden Kite Award from the Society of Children's Book Writers & Illustrators and the PEN Center West Award for Children's Literature. A longtime volunteer at the Humane Society, she often uses animals in her stories.

Peg and her husband, Carl, live in a log house on ten acres of forest near Mount Rainer National Park. Their property is a sanctuary for blacktail deer, elk, rabbits, and many kinds of birds. They have two grown children, four grandchildren, a dog, and a cat. When she is not writing, Peg likes to read, watch baseball and gymnastics, and pump her old player piano.